FIRST
STRIKE

A Brady Hawk novel

R.J.
PATTERSON

First Strike
© Copyright 2016 R.J. Patterson

Cover Design by Books Covered

Published in the United States of America
Green E-Books
Boise Idaho 83713

What Others Are Saying
about R.J. Patterson

"R.J. Patterson does a fantastic job at keeping you engaged and interested. I look forward to more from this talented author."

- Aaron Patterson
bestselling author of SWEET DREAMS

DEAD SHOT

"Small town life in southern Idaho might seem quaint and idyllic to some. But when local newspaper reporter Cal Murphy begins to uncover a series of strange deaths that are linked to a sticky spider web of deception, the lid on the peaceful town is blown wide open. Told with all the energy and bravado of an old pro, first-timer R.J. Patterson hits one out of the park his first time at bat with *Dead Shot*. It's that good."

- Vincent Zandri
bestselling author of THE REMAINS

"You can tell R.J. knows what it's like to live in the newspaper world, but with *Dead Shot*, he's proven that he also can write one heck of a murder mystery."

- Josh Katzowitz
NFL writer for CBSSports.com
& author of Sid Gillman: Father of the Passing Game

"Patterson has a mean streak about a mile wide and puts his two main characters through quite a horrible ride, which makes for good reading."

- Richard D., reader

DEAD LINE

"This book kept me on the edge of my seat the whole time. I didn't really want to put it down. R.J. Patterson has hooked me. I'll be back for more."

- Bob Behler
3-time Idaho broadcaster of the year
and play-by-play voice for Boise State football

"Like a John Grisham novel, from the very start I was pulled right into the story and couldn't put the book down. It was as if I personally knew and cared about what happened to each of the main characters. Every chapter ended with so much excitement and suspense I had to continue to read until I learned how it ended, even though it kept me up until 3:00 A.M.

- Ray F., reader

DEAD IN THE WATER

"In Dead in the Water, R.J. Patterson accurately captures the action-packed saga of a what could be a real-life college football scandal. The sordid details will leave readers flipping through the pages as fast as a hurry-up offense."

- Mark Schlabach,
ESPN college sports columnist and
co-author of *Called to Coach*
and *Heisman: The Man Behind the Trophy*

THE WARREN OMISSIONS

"What can be more fascinating than a super high concept novel that reopens the conspiracy behind the JFK assassination while the threat of a global world war rests in the balance? With his new novel, *The Warren Omissions*, former journalist turned bestselling author R.J. Patterson proves he just might be the next worthy successor to Vince Flynn."

- Vincent Zandri
bestselling author of THE REMAINS

OTHER TITLES BY
R.J. PATTERSON

Cal Murphy Thrillers
Dead Shot
Dead Line
Better off Dead
Dead in the Water
Dead Man's Curve
Dead and Gone
Dead Wrong
Dead Man's Land
Dead to Rights
Dead End

James Flynn Thrillers
The Warren Omissions
Imminent Threat
The Cooper Affair
Seeds of War

Brady Hawk Thrillers
First Strike
Deep Cover
Point of Impact
Full Blast
Target Zero
Fury
State of Play
Siege

For Sean, a real American hero

CHAPTER 0

Present Day
Zaranj, Afghanistan

BRADY HAWK JAMMED a clip into his P226 pistol and set it down on the dusty table. He stared at it for a second, pondering the twisted path that led him to this moment, the one where he geared himself up to go on a killing spree. The last time he'd been in this godforsaken part of the world he was helping people in a substantial way—not masquerading as an English teacher, but getting down in the sand and helping the people who needed it most. This time his help was less tangible but far more important.

Hawk concluded the only thing that had really changed was his tactics. Digging wells and teaching people different methods of irrigation *were* helpful, but it was useless if they were about to be killed by 21st Century marauders who conjured up the spirit of Genghis Kahn. He'd help them again more tangibly in due time. But in the world now, there were more pressing matters—specifically, a terrorist group named Al Hasib.

Hawk stepped over the dead body in the middle of his kitchen and strode toward the bathroom. Hawk brushed the dust off the mirror and stared at the man in front of him. Despite his reluctance, his eyes went directly to the scar on the right side of his forehead, a constant reminder of why he was here. His scraggly beard fell well past his neck, a symbol of his feeble attempt to blend into life here. Despite his disdain for the region's troublemakers, he'd managed to temper his anger, hiding in plain sight—until now. He picked up a pair of scissors from the ledge of the bathroom sink and hacked away at the hair dangling beneath his chin. His razor quickly followed, leaving him with a clean-shaven face.

His deep blue eyes stared back at him, half urging him onward in his mission and half begging him to return to the safe life he could have in the United States. Given who his father was, Hawk would've never been extended an opportunity to join Firestorm, the black ops team comprised of elite ex-military soldiers. With a father as a world-renowned weapons maker, Hawk could become a liability, a public symbol that Al Hasib, or any other terrorist group, would love to behead as a statement. But Hawk was *that* good. So good in fact that Senator J.D. Blunt, the senior official from Texas who oversaw the program, personally signed off on allowing Hawk to join the team.

"The upside far outweighs the downside," argued Blunt as he chewed on an unlit cigar before the rest of the Firestorm committee. "He may strike more precisely than a thousand drone bombings."

Blunt's confidence in Hawk only fueled his passion to prove the senator right—not that Hawk needed any. Motivation was as plentiful as the desert sand. But he didn't want to think about it. It was too painful, too real. It had been three years, but the wound hadn't even scabbed over. Every day he awoke to the image of Emily facing her executioners in Deir ez-Zor along the banks of the Euphrates River. It was the enduring image he saw every time before he locked in to assassin mode and began killing with precision.

Hawk returned to the kitchen and collected all his weapons on the table, strapping them to his person. The dead body lying prone in front of him wasn't even cold, but he was far from being done killing for the night. He was just getting started, as he was finally ready to do what he'd gone to Zaranj to do: Kill Nasim Ghazi.

CHAPTER 1

Two Months Earlier
Kirkuk, Iraq

HAWK HUSTLED UP THE STEPS flanking the back of the two-story adobe home. Staying low, he wormed his way along the rooftop until he reached his perch. The sun directly overhead had warmed the air but not the rooftop. It only felt mildly warm to his elbows. He turned on his comlink and dug out his binoculars.

"Tell me what I'm looking at here," Hawk said.

"I hope you're looking at the U.S. consulate in Kirkuk," replied Alex Duncan, Hawk's sassy handler. She was a CIA reject, an analyst-turned-handler who lost her job a year ago because she bucked the system one too many times. With some time off to reflect on her missteps that led to her ouster, she had a firm grasp on why discretion was truly the better part of valor. Instead of growing bitter, she decided to change her attitude—though she wasn't completely reformed.

She still believed rules *could* be broken if necessary, a long way from her previous belief that rules were *made* to be broken. The combination made her the perfect handler for an ops program like Firestorm.

"Kirkuk? I thought I was supposed to be in Baghdad," he deadpanned.

"Cut the comedy act, Hawk. I'm watching you on a satellite feed," she said.

He tweaked the focus on his binoculars. "You know I've never understood these terrorists, killing themselves for an ideology they'll never live to see realized."

"It's not much different than anyone who volunteers to go to war."

"But when you go to war, at least you do so with the hope that you'll come home and see the ideal for which you fought for come to life."

Alex waited for a moment before responding. "I always believed there were two kinds of men in the world—men who go to their deaths screaming, and men who go to their deaths in silence. Then I met a third kind."

Hawk pulled his binoculars back. "Wait a minute. Are you quoting Mr. McKinley from *Rang De Basanti*? I had no idea you were into Bollywood films."

"You know, I'm not sure if I like working with you any more now."

"Why's that?"

"Because all my nuggets of wisdom come from Bollywood films, and I don't know if I can have someone outing me as a fraudulent philosopher."

"If you quit because of that, you're going to miss out on exploring my extensive Bollywood DVD collection. I only loan out my movies to work friends."

She laughed. "You see anything going on out there yet?"

He smiled and pressed his binoculars against his face. He zoomed in on the consulate. "Not much going on, but the building is still smoldering."

"I can see that, too."

"You know, Alex, this is the third mission you've sent me on where I'm convinced you could've done the same thing from your office. I love the frequent mileage points, but this isn't exactly what I signed up for."

"No one ever signs up for what they get. It's called life."

"Are you always this cranky this late at night?"

"There's something about smart asses that brings it out in me. Besides, it's more like early morning in my book." She paused. "So, you can't see anything?"

"Apparently, not much more than you can. Just a few armed guards milling around. It's time for the Zuhr prayer here—just not a lot going on right now."

"You're going to need to get closer."

Hawk scanned the structure again with his binoculars. "How close?"

"Inside."

"Inside? So I'm going from casual observer to infiltrating a heavily guarded compound on my own?"

"Exactly. Isn't that what you signed up for?"

Before he could answer, a gunshot cracked through the air and a bullet whizzed past him. Hawk stayed low and scrambled behind an air conditioning unit a few meters away.

"A heads up would've been nice," Hawk said as he pulled out his gun and glanced in the direction the shot came from. Another bullet whistled past him.

"I've got a delay of a few seconds here."

Hawk rolled over to the other side of the air conditioning unit and snuck a peek toward the gunfire. Nothing. "Can you give me some help here?"

"I see it now," she said. "You've got what looks like a single shooter three rooftops away to the east."

"Any way out of here?"

"There's a van in the alleyway behind you. You could jump and land on it. Shouldn't be too far of a fall. And I don't think the shooter is in a position where he could see you."

"Think or know? This isn't the time for conjecture."

"Know."

"Roger that."

Hawk slithered backward and dropped off the edge of the roof onto the van. He slid down and headed toward the shooter.

"What are you doing?" Alex asked. "You need to get out of there."

"No, what I need are answers—like how did someone know I was here and who sent this guy to kill me."

"You know you're on your own if you get caught."

"Yeah, I know that as well as I know my own name and my alias."

Hawk could hear her sigh.

"I don't know how well I can help you now," she said. "There's a delay in my feed, remember?"

"Do what you can."

Hawk stopped and pointed at a set of steps leading to what he guessed was the rooftop three houses away. He waited for Alex's response.

"That's the one," she said.

Hawk crept up the first flight of stairs, keeping his body flush with the wall. The second flight started at the corner and ascended to the roof.

"Hawk!" Alex screamed. "He's heading straight for—"

Hawk was not only five seconds ahead of her, but he was two steps ahead as well. He'd taken the comlink out of his left ear and could hear the faint footfalls of the man descending the steps. Hawk recoiled and delivered a blow to the man's throat as he turned the corner. With the man gasping for air and unable to scream, Hawk smashed the man's face with his knee. The crack of a broken nose echoed in the alleyway.

Undaunted by the beating he was taking, the man attempted to fight back, swinging weakly at Hawk. Annoyed by the gesture, Hawk head butted the man and sent him falling backward into the alley from a height of no more than four meters.

Hawk raced toward the man, who wasn't moving. He felt for a pulse. *Still kicking.*

"Are you all right?" Alex asked after her feed caught up with the man falling into the alley.

"Never better."

"He's not much good to you now, is he?"

Hawk shook his head. "Let's see who you are." He started digging around in the man's pocket and found a set of keys and a picture—a picture of Hawk. "Now this just got really interesting."

"What?"

"Alex, he has a picture of me on him. And it's a picture of me from when I was in Syria working with the Peace Corps. Please tell me how this guy has this."

"I don't have time."

"Really? It's not a difficult question to answer. You either know or you don't."

"Hawk! Listen to me. Prayers are ending. You need to get out of there now. People are returning to the streets."

He stared at the man and knelt down and tucked the photo into his back pocket. "Screw it. I'm taking him with me."

"In broad daylight? Are you out of your mind?"

Hawk hoisted the man's limp body onto his shoulders. "I've got to get my answers one way or another." Hawk tugged on his keffiyeh and swung the excess material across his face. He glanced beyond the alley and into the street with his would-be assassin in tow.

"That's not a good idea, Hawk," Alex said in his ear.

"You got a better one?" Hawk strode across the street.

He started to open the back of his Land Rover when a man carrying an assault rifle spotted Hawk and yelled at him in Arabic. Left vulnerable, Hawk had no other option except to drop his prisoner and use the Land Rover as a shield. Hawk nonchalantly nodded at the man before dumping the assassin's body on the ground. Hawk yanked the driver's side door open and jumped behind the steering wheel, twisting the key in the ignition as the engine roared to life.

Hawk stomped on the gas, kicking up a small storm of dust—but not before the gunman in the street fired a few shots in his direction, one of which hit the side of the Land Rover.

"What the hell is going on, Hawk?" Alex's voice crackled through his comlink.

"Nothing to worry about. I've got it all under control."

"That's not what it looks like from here," she snapped.

"Looks can be deceiving."

"Yeah —you *look* sane."

"We've got far bigger problems to worry about than my sanity—like a traitor in our midst."

Hawk rounded the corner and jammed his foot on the brakes, bringing his vehicle to a skidding stop. With a large black SUV in front of him, he turned around and looked over his shoulder while shifting the car into reverse. Before he could step on the gas, another SUV backed out of the alleyway and boxed him in. Several armed men stormed out of the vehicles and surrounded him.

"Hawk!" Alex said. "What's going on?"

He sat in the car with his arms raised. "I'm surrounded."

CHAPTER 2

SENATOR J.D. BLUNT GNAWED on an unlit cigar for a moment before looking at the wiry freshman senator from the Defense Budget Committee across the long conference room table. Meetings that started at 7 a.m. always put him in a foul mood before the first word was ever uttered. But the subject that convened that particular gathering would've made his blood boil no matter when it started.

He slowly removed the cigar from his mouth with his middle and index finger on his right hand and took a deep breath. He put his head down and glared at the man.

"I'm sorry, Senator," Blunt said as he snapped his fingers. "What's your name again?"

"Hirschbeck. Guy Hirschbeck."

"Senator Herschel," Blunt began, purposefully butchering his fellow senator's name, "I don't think I heard what you just said quite right."

Hirschbeck straightened his tie and glanced down

at the paper on the table in front of him. "I said I recommend ending Project Z, whatever that is. All I know is that it's a black hole in the defense budget. Perhaps it's your discretionary fund for all those trips you take to the Bahamas with your aides." He paused. "You know, the ones you used to take without your wife Carolyn."

Blunt leaned back in his chair and smiled. He pointed at Hirschbeck with his cigar. "You know, Huffman, I like you. You've got a lot of gumption."

Hirschbeck glared at the man. "The people didn't elect me to become popular with the rest of congress—they elected me to clean up the wasteful spending people like you are making."

Blunt stood and stuffed the cigar in his mouth. He then leaned forward, resting his knuckles on the table. "You really wanna take a run at me, son? You better bring it. This project that you know nothing about—and never will—is what's keeping you safe at night. I suggest you back off before you learn the hard way that serving on the defense committee isn't about winning approval ratings from the people but about doing what's necessary to keep them safe."

"We have laws, Senator, and—"

"We also have madmen running around in the Middle East who want to destroy this country, and every time one of our drones drops a bomb on them, five terrorists are born for every one we kill. Project Z is not only more effective militarily but also politically. If you want to try and pull the plug, go ahead. But there will be consequences for you."

Hirschbeck swallowed hard. "Are you threatening me?"

Blunt sat down and clasped his hands together. "I never make threats—only promises."

***

BLUNT TOSSED A STACK of papers on his desk and pulled out a bottle of bourbon from his bottom right drawer. He didn't see his chief aide, Hunter Preston, follow him into his office.

"A little early to be drinking, isn't it?" Preston said.

Blunt ignored the question and kept pouring a generous portion. "It's a little late for me when I have to deal with jerk wads like Hasselman."

"It's Hirschbeck, sir. And I suggest you learn his name because he's not going away any time soon."

Blunt took a long pull on his drink. "We need to dig up some dirt on him, make him resign in disgrace."

"Sir, with all due respect, isn't this the game you played last time that ended up with your exploits to the Caribbean made public?"

Blunt grunted and swallowed another swig. "The good people of Texas are a forgiving bunch. There aren't any more skeletons in the closet for them to dig up—well, at least there aren't the kind that would make my constituency turn against me." He paused and stared out the window. "Did you need something?"

"Yes, General Johnson needs to speak with you. There's been a development. He said it's urgent."

Blunt nodded and dismissively waved his hand at Preston. Once his aide closed the door, Blunt dialed Johnson, the general tasked with leading Project Z, or for those in the know, Firestorm. General Johnson was hardly more than a figurehead required to get approval on all missions involving Brady Hawk. The program's two other special operatives were less active and used only as a replacement for Hawk if something should happen to him or if he was preoccupied. Blunt was the one actually in charge of the scope of Firestorm while Johnson managed the handlers, oversaw the daily administrative tasks, and helped plan missions.

"What's going on? I'm facing a shit storm here with a nosy little freshman senator," Blunt said.

Johnson sighed. "We've got bigger problems."

"Such as?"

"Such as we just lost contact with our top asset

in the field. I wanted to see if you could possibly call in a favor for me and see if we can find out where he is and get an extraction team together to pull him out."

Blunt drummed his fingers on the desk. "I told you when this started that you and your team were on your own, and I still mean it. No calls. No favors. If he can't figure a way out, he obviously wasn't the right man for the job."

"But Senator—"

"Figure out another way or let him twist in the wind. Whatever got him caught, he should've been more careful."

"How do you expect me to run a program like this?"

"Very carefully." He paused. "Besides, regardless of what happens to our asset, everything is going as planned."

CHAPTER 3

ALEX DUNCAN HAD TYPED FURIOUSLY on her keyboard, trying to reposition the few satellites she could maneuver. The last transmission she saw revealed a chilling image—Hawk boxed in and surrounded with his last hopeless words echoing in her mind. *I'm surrounded.*

But when the satellites came into the proper position, Hawk was gone. So was his Land Rover, along with every one else. The street was quiet, devoid of even a trace of human activity.

She continued her search with the satellites but knew there wouldn't be much chance of finding Hawk, if any. After several hours of fruitless monitoring the bank of screens in front of her, she decided to get a few hours of sleep. She awoke at 5:30 a.m. and waited until a reasonable hour to report Hawk's situation to Senator Blunt. But since she told him what happened, she hadn't heard a word.

Damn it, Hawk! If you'd have just listened to me.

She needed coffee—a gallon of it, at least. Locking up her office, she wandered down the street toward her favorite diner, The Golden Egg. After she took a seat at the counter, she said hello to her favorite chef, Cookie, and didn't even have to place an order. Cookie slid a full mug of black coffee in front of her and rattled off her usual order: scrambled eggs, hash browns, buttery grits, two crisp pieces of bacon, and wheat toast. The wheat toast made her feel like she was at least making an attempt to eat healthy. It was a lie she happily told herself and tried desperately to believe it.

I'll run it off at the gym.

She grabbed a copy of *The Washington Post* that had been abandoned on the seat next to her. "Congress Debates Refugee Policy" blared the headline above the fold. She shook her head.

If people only knew what really goes on in this town …

She flipped the pages until she reached the "Beltway Roundup" section that covered all the ins and outs of what was happening among the D.C. elite. That's when she saw his picture—Simon Coker, the head of the CIA, the man who oversaw her firing. His mere image dredged up painful memories she would've rather remained buried deep within the recesses of her mind.

"If you're not okay with how we do things here,

perhaps it's time you see your way out and never come back," Coker had told her in their last face-to-face meeting.

She'd demanded to see him, upset over the interrogation tactics she witnessed with a suspected terrorist. She confronted him, warning that she had a copy of the torture and would leak it to the press if he didn't change the way the agency conducted interrogations in the future. He ignored her and promised her that if she did such a thing, she'd experience something far worse.

Their back and forth lasted for less than a minute before he had her escorted off the premises, never to return. She didn't even have a chance to retrieve the thumb drive she'd copied the interrogation on. A rookie mistake on her part, one she vowed never to make again—a vow that manifested itself through her meticulous record keeping. All the shoeboxes full of thumb drives scattered throughout her house since she started working for Firestorm proved that she had indeed taken her promise seriously.

However, that new habit didn't help Alex in her immediate plight following her firing from the CIA. Coker's vendetta against her was so strong that he manipulated her records to the point that it was nearly impossible for her to get a job. She came home one day to find a bouquet of flowers on her apartment steps with a note that read, "Here's a gift card for Mc-Donald's. Perhaps you can apply for a job there and they'll take you." It was signed "SC".

She went inside her apartment and proceeded to break most of her dishes in a fit of rage. In just over two years, she went from joining the CIA to being broke and destitute. It was a stunning turn of events for Alex, who'd always dreamed of being a spy since she learned the truth about her mother. When she was seventeen, she came across some documents in her parents' attic and learned that her mother was a spy for the KGB. Her mother admitted that it was only partially true—she was a double spy, feeding benign information back to Moscow while divulging key secrets to the CIA.

But one of the field agents Blunt recruited had also worked with Alex at the CIA and recommended he talk to her. Her acumen as a handler and analyst was exactly what Blunt needed. She'd maneuvered around Coker's blackball and decided she wasn't going to waste a second chance at spycraft. Yet there she was. On her fourth mission with Firestorm, she'd lost Hawk.

Her phone buzzed on the counter next to her. It was Blunt.

"It's not your fault," he said after she answered. "Hawk should've stuck to the mission."

"That *was* the mission," she said before mouthing "thank you" to Cookie who'd just put a hot breakfast plate in front of her.

"Don't try to defend him," Blunt said. "It looks better for you to admit that he went rogue."

She sighed. "I told him to get out of there before prayers ended."

"Hawk's gonna do what Hawk's gonna do. Just keep looking for him. Don't worry. He'll contact us when he gets the opportunity."

She inhaled her food and slapped a generous tip on the counter.

"Thanks, Cookie," she said, grabbing the copy of *The Washington Post* and turning toward the door.

Despite her suspicious nature, she never noticed the man sitting in the back corner who got up when she left and followed her outside.

CHAPTER 4

THE SMELL OF BURLAP overwhelmed Hawk as he took a deep breath and struggled to free himself of the bindings around his wrists, which bound him to a wooden chair. Even if he could free himself, he wasn't sure he wanted to see what awaited him. Armed guards? An explosive device? A sword-wielding man? He couldn't imagine a single pleasant image on the other side of the sack tied snuggly around his head. So he stopped trying and decided to save his strength.

I bet Alex is freaking out right now.

Just the thought made him smile. He knew she liked him. Call it instinct—or experience—but he just knew. Despite baiting her, he knew getting her to profess her love for him over the coms would be next to impossible. And he wouldn't give her a shred of hope until he met her face to face. There was only so much you could learn about a person by talking over a long distance. The face-to-face meeting was crucial—and it wasn't about looks either, though if Hawk was honest with himself, he knew it was around twenty-five percent about looks. The rest, however, was about chemistry. And while they seemed to have chemistry on their missions, he wouldn't know for sure until he spent some time with her in person. He needed to look into her eyes, touch her hand, smell her perfume. He needed to see if she could jam or had two left feet when his favorite Michael Jackson song—"Don't Stop 'Til You Get Enough"—came on the radio. He needed to watch her as she answered his questions—the personal kind.

Just thinking about Alex gave him the distraction he needed to avoid dwelling on the reality of his current situation—hands tied behind his back to a chair with a sack secured around his head.

Hawk jolted back to reality when he heard a door slam across the room. A guard removed the sack on Hawk's head and then exited. He peered into the room, struggling to adjust to the sudden flood of light. Repeatedly squeezing his eyes shut and then opening them, his surroundings began to come into focus—and it was a more dire situation than he hoped. Armed guards stood near the door. Tall and muscular, they looked like they'd used their weapons plenty in the past. Then another man entered the room right behind them. He wasn't carrying a gun, but he had something in his hand.

"He's all yours," the guard said before leaving through the only door.

Two guards accompanied the latecomer as he strode across the floor toward Hawk. The man brandished a knife, scraping it lightly across his thumb as he stared down his prisoner. Initially, Hawk didn't recognize the man—but it was clear he was the one in charge.

Hawk scanned the room, identifying three exit points, the least desirable being the door they'd just entered. How heavily guarded it was and where it led remained a mystery, but the two opaque windows on each side of the large room shielded the bright sunlight. Wherever they led, it was into an open area outside. There were still plenty of unknown variables, but he liked his chances there as opposed to an unknown corridor.

As the man walked toward Hawk, he didn't flinch. If they'd wanted him dead, he'd already be dead. And in the off chance that they only wanted to keep him alive for propaganda purposes, he sure as hell wasn't about to read some radical diatribe before they chopped his head off. Hawk figured his death would be short and sweet, though he lamented the fact that he'd die without ever drinking another pint of his favorite scotch.

"Mister Hawk," the man began, "it seems we have something in common."

"What? We both don't mind killing another man?"

The man furrowed his brow and glared at Hawk. "Is this sarcasm? I never quite had a knack for picking up on it when I studied at UCLA."

"Now, we definitely don't have as much in common as you think. I'm a Trojan, and we Trojans hate Bruins."

The man closed his eyes and shook his head, annoyed at Hawk's attempts at humor. "This isn't comedy hour, Mr. Hawk."

"Well, it sure ain't a day at the spa either," Hawk snapped.

"Perhaps I should start over. My name is Rasul Moradi, and I understand we have a common enemy—one that I'd rather see dead."

Hawk looked off in the distance at the two guards who'd entered with Moradi. Half listening to his captor, he tried to calculate his chances of escape while he surveyed the other men in the room.

I'd put it at 10-1 that I don't make it. And I like those odds.

"Does the name Nasim Ghazi sound familiar to you?" Moradi asked.

Hawk slowly returned his gaze to Moradi. It did indeed. Nasim Ghazi was the whole reason he was in Kirkuk, tracking down Al Hasib's chief bomb maker.

He couldn't strike without being there, and Firestorm wanted eyes on him to develop a plan to take him out. If the powers that presided over Firestorm had their way, Ghazi's death would appear as an accident so as to avoid a retaliatory backlash. The rumor was that Ghazi liked to admire his work, often returning to the scene to study how the bomb exploded in an effort to better place the next bomb he detonated. Ghazi had just struck the U.S. Consulate in Kirkuk, and Hawk had been dispatched within minutes after it happened to look for the infamous bomb maker. If he got close enough to kill the man somehow and make it look like an accident, all the better. As long as Hawk could see Ghazi, all would be well, and for the time being, Ghazi was off doing who knew what, plotting against any number of Al Hasib's enemies.

"I've heard of him," Hawk said. "What do you want with him?"

"Same as you, I suppose," Moradi said as he looked at the ground. Then he looked up. "I want him dead."

"And why's that?"

"Let's just say it's personal."

"What?" Hawk said, feigning not hearing.

Moradi bent over and got right in Hawk's face. "I said, 'It's personal'."

Hawk eased back in his chair before jerking forward violently. He cracked Moradi's nose, sending him sprawling on the ground in pain. Hawk rolled over and whipped his chair against the floor, shattering it as his bindings loosened. He worked to get free as the guards rushed toward the commotion about fifteen meters away.

In one swift move, Hawk shook the ropes free and rolled onto the floor next to Moradi, who writhed in agony. Hawk pulled Moradi's gun from his holster and used his former captor as a human shield. He knelt down and picked up Moradi's knife as well, shoving it in his pocket.

"That's far enough," Hawk said to the guards as he held a gun to Moradi's head. The two guards appeared confused until Moradi ordered them in Arabic to put down their weapons.

In a perfect situation, Hawk would've wasted the two guards and Moradi too. But this was far from perfect with the element of the unknown making him hesitant to develop a solid plan. Taking risks in a familiar environment was one thing, but rushing in blind with no support was foolish. He ordered the guards to sit against a pole along the edge of the wall. Quickly, Hawk worked to secure them to the pole with the rope that had just held him moments ago. He then ripped part of their shirts and created a makeshift gag.

Hawk put his finger to his lips. "Ssshhh."

"Seems like you have a—" Moradi gasped for a breath "—problem."

Hawk glanced over to see Moradi holding out his wrists after watching Hawk use the last shred of rope to bind the guards. Hawk eyed Moradi closely while he stood. "I prefer to call them challenges, and you won't like how I've solved this one." He rushed toward Moradi and grabbed him from behind, placing him in a sleeper hold.

"I don't work with terrorists," Hawk said before Moradi's body finally went limp.

Moradi wouldn't be out more than five minutes, but Hawk figured if he couldn't escape Moradi's compound during that time, it wouldn't matter anyway because Hawk would probably be dead.

Hawk turned his attention to his next challenge—getting through the window that was three meters off the ground. It measured about a meter square, providing plenty of room for him to wriggle through the pane that appeared to slide upward. Hawk grabbed a crate from the corner of the room and stepped on it as he opened the window.

In the central court of the compound, a flurry of activity took place. Several guards hustled back and forth between two trucks with covered beds, transferring wooden crates. In the far corner, two guards roamed in front of a chain link fence that looked like the main entrance in and out of the grounds. He looked in the other direction and saw a lone guard roaming around the perimeter of presumably the back wall.

Hawk surveyed the situation for a minute until he saw his opportunity. One of the guards called several of the men over to look at a magazine. Hawk couldn't quite make out what magazine it was, but he could see that there was a scantily-clad woman on the front. The men smiled and pointed, laughing as they leered at the pictures inside. One of the guards snatched the magazine and then turned it sideways, much to the delight of the other men. With everyone distracted by the magazine, and the transfer activity completed, Hawk slithered through the window and down to the ground. Keeping low, he hustled about ten meters toward the truck and jumped inside. He tucked himself behind a row of wooden crates and waited.

Less than a few minutes later, the truck roared to life and started to rumble along a dirt road laden with pot holes. After two minutes, the truck moved onto a main road, barreling to some destination. Hawk pried open one of the crates with Moradi's knife and sifted through the contents—a slew of unarmed IEDs.

Without hesitating, Hawk cut wire after wire on both ends of the connections, rendering the IEDs useless. They could be repaired, but not without a considerable amount of work. And if he got lucky, the shipment would be to some terrorist who was bigger and badder than Moradi and take offense at an apparent attempt at deception, and they would require restitution. But Hawk wasn't interested in sticking around to find out.

The truck lurched forward and jerked to a stop, sending several of the crates sliding. A piece of paper still lodged beneath one of the crates caught his eye. He leaned over and picked it up.

What's this?

Hawk stared, mouth agape, at the piece of paper before folding it up and shoving it in his pocket.

A few minutes later, he recognized that they were rolling through the heart of Kirkuk. Once the truck stopped at a crowded intersection, he slipped out the back and disappeared.

Wasting no time, he made his way to a pay phone and called Alex.

"Hawk?" she said. "You're alive. I thought we lost you."

"Lose me?" he said with a chuckle. "Never. But you won't believe what I found."

CHAPTER 5

SENATOR BLUNT LUMBERED onto the stage in the large lecture hall at the Elliott School of International Affairs. George Washington University's reputation as one of the best foreign affairs programs in the nation was bolstered by its easy access to experts on the subject just minutes down the street. Blunt was a regular speaker in the school's popular Middle East Policy Forum where he often debated weak-kneed politicians who wanted the country to return to a more isolationist policy.

"What do they think? Al Hasib is going to sit down at a table over a glass of wine, sing 'Kumbaya', and solve the world's problems?" Blunt once groused to Preston after eviscerating a freshman senator on stage. "And to think there were people dumb enough to actually agree with him that diplomacy will work with these nut jobs. The day these millennial snowflakes take over the country, it's over."

That afternoon, Blunt took hold of the lectern,

unopposed. And he was about to use his bully pulpit to reiterate what he'd been preaching for the last fifteen years—that until the rest of the world ferreted out and destroyed the Islamic radicals threatening their freedom, the rats were only going to reproduce with each generation, becoming more vicious than the previous one.

He shuffled his papers, which were little more than a prop. Blunt didn't need to memorize a speech or even prepare one, for that matter. Eliminating radical groups like Al Hasib was what drove him to push for Firestorm and finagle his way into the leadership role. His ranking of general in the Army qualified him as such, not to mention it made for a less complicated line of communication. Once he traded enough votes with fellow congressional leaders to secure the job, he hired an all-star staff who understood what it took to get the job done. Finding rogue agents to work on black ops missions wasn't as difficult as he thought it would be, and he knew he'd found a couple of jewels with Alex Duncan as a handler and Brady Hawk as his chief reconnaissance officer. Of course, Hawk had other pertinent skills necessary to complete other subsidiary missions.

On the screen in the background, a stark blue background provided contrast for the bold white letters of his lecture's title: "Why Diplomacy in the Middle East Fails". For the next half hour, he offered his standard drumbeat—one that inspired war hawks and angered the peace doves.

"The biggest problem we make in the West is that we assume the rulers in the Middle East want peace. They don't. They want war, the kind that—if they win—will lead to world domination guided by a religion that is at odds with almost everything we believe," Blunt said, pounding the lectern periodically to make an even greater emphasis. "If anything, it stands diametrically opposed to the Constitution and the principles upon which this country was founded. And if we try to appease them, we're going to wake up one day wondering how these countries managed to find a way to bring the war to U.S. soil. And it'll be a day where we rue the pacifist doctrines we've tried to implement in our foreign policy."

Once Blunt concluded his lecture, hands flew up around the room. He shifted his weight from one foot to the next until he decided which student he would call upon first. A young man with a beard and a tie-dyed shirt emblazoned with a peace symbol received Blunt's permissive nod.

"You, sir," Blunt said. "What's your question?"

"Isn't it short-sighted to think that many of the Middle Eastern countries won't change, and by continuing these aggressive foreign policies, the U.S.

government is only perpetrating your ideological stance by making generational enemies?" the young man asked.

Blunt sighed and shook his head. "If you think the idea of world domination isn't the end game of these leaders, you need to go back and re-read history. As soon as those countries started gaining wealth and diplomatic power, they began their assault on our freedoms. If you think it's bad now, it's going to get much worse—mark my word."

The young man stood back up. "You didn't answer my question."

Blunt glared at him. "I'm sorry. I didn't realize you were only looking for a terse response. So, in short, my answer is no, it's not short-sighted, and it doesn't perpetrate anything."

He held his hands up as he walked off the stage. "Sorry, that's all the time I have for questions."

The professor who invited Blunt shook his hand and thanked him for coming.

"I don't know how you put up with a classroom full of kids who don't know how to think critically," Blunt said. "And I thought trying to reason with Congress was a difficult task."

Blunt turned toward Preston, who had remained in the wings for the duration of the speech.

"Good speech, sir," Preston said.

"Next time I'll let you give it. How many times have you heard me give that speech? Ten? Twenty?"

"I hear it every day."

Blunt chuckled. "I wish these little prima donnas would not only hear it but take it to heart. Perhaps if we made a video game where you could only unlock the next level if you understood a basic grasp of the reality of the world we live in—"

"They'd only look for hacks on the Internet to get to the next level. Your best intentions would be lost on them."

Blunt and Preston walked toward a back exit in an effort to avoid a confrontation with one of the students. A few years before, one had tried to entrap Blunt with a question that resulted in a viral video that brought a minor embarrassment to him. Fortunately, it wasn't during an election year, so it didn't become an issue. But Blunt vowed to never put himself in such a vulnerable environment again.

Before they reached the door, a young woman stepped into their path.

"Excuse me, Senator, but I was wondering if I might have a moment of your time," she said.

Blunt side-stepped her as he waved at her dismissively. "Got a country to help run, ma'am. Maybe another time."

"So, you don't want to comment on the secret

CIA program, which is the focus of my expose later this month in *The Washington Post*?"

He turned around. "I don't know what you're talking about, but I would advise you to stop poking around where you don't belong."

She flashed a quick smirk. "Poking around is what I do."

"Well, just be careful not to poke the bear." He turned his back and continued toward the door.

"My name is Madeline Meissner, Senator. That's Meissner with two esses. You'll be hearing from me again."

Blunt leaned over and whispered to Preston. "Take care of her, will you?"

CHAPTER 6

ALEX DUNCAN BARELY HEARD a word Hawk said as she exhaled, relieved that he not only was still alive, but also out of the hands of terrorists. She hammered away on her keyboard, typing out an email to Blunt with an update.

"Alex?" A pause. "Alex? Are you listening to me?" Hawk said.

"Still here. Just preoccupied at the moment."

"What can be more important than what I just told you?"

"Well, the fact that you're alive, and people want to know. That's pretty damn important, if you ask me."

"Now I know you weren't listening to me."

She sighed. "Okay. I'm listening. What is so much more important than the well-being of this program's best-placed asset in the field?"

"I am replaceable, you know."

"I doubt that. Now will you please just tell me

what you were yammering on about while I was letting my boss know that you're still alive."

"What I said was, 'You won't believe what I found'."

"Don't keep me in suspense, Hawk. Just out with it already."

"Okay, while I was riding in the back of this covered truck, I found a note from Karif Fazil."

"The leader of Al Hasib?"

"The one and only. Apparently, he and Rasul Moradi had a falling out, but it had to be after this note."

"Wait. Back up. Rasul Moradi? Am I supposed to know who he is?"

"He's the small-time arms dealer that just took me hostage. Look him up. He's not a big player in the scope of world terrorism, but he's linked to plenty of terrorists who have blown up their share of buildings."

"So, how does that note help us?"

"It lists the coordinates for where Moradi's group is supposed to drop off weapons for Al Hasib."

"Okay. Give them to me so I can find out what we might be able to do with them."

"No drone strikes. Just promise me that."

"I'll make sure I pass the word along."

"The last thing we need is to make more terrorists. Besides, I want to do some reconnaissance on these sites."

Alex took down the coordinates and forwarded them along to Blunt. Reluctantly, she added Hawk's plea that there shouldn't be any drone strikes, but she doubted he'd listen. If Blunt was intent on annihilating something, he would do it and apologize later. It wasn't as if her boss took too kindly to anybody telling him what to do—not even the President.

"Check in tomorrow," Alex said as she typed. "I'll have your next assignment for you."

"Don't bother. I know what needs to be done. I'm going dark, and I'll contact you when I resurface."

"And where are you going?"

"To gather more intel on Al Hasib's hideout in the mountains."

"I guess there's no use in trying to persuade you to wait, is there?"

"Nope."

"Blunt won't like this."

"Screw him. If he wants the best intel available, I can't sit around waiting for him to tell me what I already know I need to do. I've got to move now."

"Good luck."

After she hung up, she called Blunt, hoping to get some sort of assignment for Hawk so she could create the illusion that Firestorm's top asset was a team player. Normally, she would just report him and let him twist in the wind. But Brady Hawk wasn't just an average agent. And if truth be told, she was fond of him—more than she should've been as his handler. Besides, it wasn't like she had any other men in her life that she cared to have any conversations with on a regular basis. Her boss, her landlord. Other than those authority figures—and Cookie—she didn't really talk to many men. It was her own fault. She was suspicious of men in general, especially after witnessing her mother's gruesome death at the hands of her father. She didn't like to talk about it—or even think about it—but it haunted her every day. Each man she saw reminded her of him.

Perhaps that's why Hawk was different. She'd never even seen him in person. To her, he was just a deep smooth voice on the other end of the phone or a comlink. When she listened to Hawk speak, she felt like the world would be just fine because he'd take care of everything. It was a fantasy, devoid of a shred of reality. Hawk simply did his job and she doubted he thought twice about her, though he might if he ever saw her.

Alex's efforts to reach Blunt resulted in nothing more than a voicemail message. She walked into the restroom before calling it a day. With her green eyes, she stared at herself in the mirror, her brown wavy hair drifting just below her shoulders. She couldn't deny how tired she looked as bags sagged beneath her eyes. Too many late nights and not enough sleep. But not tonight. She promised herself that she'd go to bed early, treat her body right. In the morning, she'd wake up refreshed and ready to take on the evil terrorists of the world.

She grabbed her bag and exited the building through the stairwell. After she'd once ended up stuck in an elevator for nearly six hours, she vowed to use the stairs for the rest of her life, no matter how many flights her destination required.

Once she reached the parking deck, she walked nonchalantly to her car. Since Firestorm was a secret program, and her office was located in a building primarily dominated by an educational non-profit, she didn't look over her shoulder as she walked toward her car. If she had, she might have seen the man who slipped up behind her.

In an instant, the man covered Alex's mouth and forced her against a pillar in the parking garage.

"Alex, I thought someone should warn you about what's going on," the man said. "Now promise me you won't scream—I'm not going to hurt you." He lifted his hand off her mouth.

She withdrew as fast as she could, resting her head against the wall. "What do you want?"

"I don't want anything other than to warn you about what you're involved in."

"What are you talking about?"

"Senator Blunt's secret program is going to get exposed, and when it does, you're going to want to be as far away from it as possible."

Alex stared him down. "Who are you?"

He waved at her dismissively. "That's not important right now. What is important is that you resign and get away from Firestorm. There will be repercussions for everyone involved, and I don't think you want that."

"I asked you a question—who are you?" Alex growled.

"Perhaps you're not listening to me," the man replied.

But before he could say another word, Alex delivered a quick uppercut to the man's face and then a swift kick to his stomach. Stunned, the man stumbled backward. She punched him twice in the face, the second hit knocking him out.

She reached into the man's pocket and fished out his wallet. "Gordon Jefferson," she said aloud as she looked at his driver's license. She smiled and tucked it back in his pocket as she dragged his body out of sight. "I bet you never saw that coming, did you?"

Alex hustled toward her car and drove away. "Gordon Jefferson?" she said. "You're going to wish you'd never messed with me."

CHAPTER 7

THE NEXT MORNING, Hawk slipped into an alleyway and knocked on a wooden door. After a few moments, a peep hole slid open and the man on the other side—Sabo Jaziri—recognized Hawk and welcomed him inside.

"Jaziri," Hawk said as he kissed the man on each cheek. "It's so good to see you."

"And you too," Jaziri replied. "I see you're doing well."

Hawk furrowed his brow. "What do you see that makes you think that?"

Jaziri shrugged. "You're alive, aren't you?"

The two men shared a hearty laugh together before Jaziri ushered his friend into the sitting room.

"Would you like some tea?" Jaziri asked. "I just finished brewing a pot."

"I'd love some," Hawk said as he settled into his chair. Jaziri hobbled out of the room briefly to fetch a pair of cups and the teapot.

"It's been a while," Jaziri said, pouring Hawk a cup with his weathered hands after he returned. "What brings you back to our beautiful country?"

Five years prior, Hawk had been assigned to a reconnaissance mission with his Navy Seal team in Kirkuk. Jaziri happened to be the CIA's well-placed asset and mission liaison, providing Hawk and the rest of the team with the intel they needed to scope out the location of an abducted journalist. Less than twenty-four hours after watching the temporary prison, Hawk's team swept in and safely recovered the journalist. Hawk saw him after that but on another mission, but it was a memory Hawk tried to suppress.

"Another reconnoissance mission," Hawk said.

"Reconnoissance or something more?"

"There's no asset to recover this time."

Jaziri took a sip of his tea and set his cup down. "Quite frankly, I never thought I'd see you again. The stories I heard about your departure from the military—"

"Don't believe everything you hear."

"And who are you working with now? I'm assuming it's not the Seals since you're alone."

"This group doesn't really have a name—well, at least not one I can tell you. Just know that it's all legitimate military activity." Hawk paused. "And I have a much larger budget."

Jaziri grinned and pick up his cup again. "Now that's what I like to hear. So what do you need?"

"Do you still have that cousin herding goats outside of Rawanduz?"

"Kejal? Yes, he's still there. But I must warn you he's not as friendly to Western ideals as I am."

Hawk leaned forward. "Does he like money?"

"Oh, very much."

"Then he's friendly enough to the Western ideals required of him."

"So, what does this mission entail?"

Hawk wagged his finger at Jaziri. "You remember the rules. The less you know, the better. Besides, it's benign, and Kejal will never be in danger as long as he keeps his mouth shut. Do you think he can do that?"

Jaziri nodded.

"When can you take me?" Hawk asked.

"Give me fifteen minutes, and I'll need to call Kejal."

"Take your time. I'm not going anywhere."

***

THE ZAGROS MOUNTAINS in the northeastern corner of Iraq conjured up mixed emotions for Hawk. It was in that rocky landscape that he had his initial epiphany that he didn't want to serve in the military ever again. While his first trip to the mountains had ended triumphantly in the safe return of an innocent civilian, his second trip made him quit the military and wonder how he ever pledged allegiance to the U.S. flag. Yet there he was on another mission. And if it were to be successful, he needed to once again suppress the memories that haunted him.

The three-hour ride from Kirkuk to Rawanduz proved to be uneventful despite the half dozen security checkpoints. Though the Islamic State of Iraq and Syria, more commonly known as ISIS, had a presence in the region, they didn't have enough forces to control the Kurdish strongholds in the mountains. The Kurds were resilient people, if nothing else, especially the ones who dominated the Zagros Mountain region. And they'd held strong against both militant radicalism and militant attacks. The checkpoints, constructed by building deep trenches to prevent car bombs and other border-crashing means, created a sense of safety in the region. Though where Hawk was about to roam, he'd only have himself—and his weapons—to rely upon for his safety.

Jaziri's truck rumbled up a winding road, ascending into one of the most scenic places in the country. The ancient art of goat herding dominated the region despite the relatively new innovation of terrace farming that had crept in over the past few years. Aside from the few modern homes dotting the hillsides, Hawk couldn't imagine the place had changed much in the past several thousand years.

After another thirty minutes of ascending the hill, they eventually reached the top and parked next to Kejal's dirt bike. Jaziri made a call, and five minutes later, Kejal shuffled toward them with his staff in hand, followed by several dozen goats.

"Before you go," Jaziri said as he started to get out of the truck, "do you have a way out?"

Hawk winked at him. "I always have a way out."

Kejal hadn't reached the truck before he began squawking at Jaziri, gesturing toward Hawk and spitting.

"What is it?" Hawk said, hoping for Jaziri to translate.

"He said he didn't know you were an American," Jaziri said.

"Tell him I just want to walk the hills with him, not teach him the words to 'Born in the USA'."

Jaziri flashed a grin. "He actually likes that song. He's a big Bruce Springsteen fan."

Hawk shrugged. "If I were to teach him the words to any song, it'd be 'Thriller'. And then he'd learn the dance."

"Oh, the Michael Jackson song. I love that one," Jaziri said, lifting his hands in the air to mimic the iconic dance.

"Whatever it takes to get him to agree to this." Hawk fished a few hundred dollar bills out of his pocket. "Maybe this will help, too." He waved the money in front of Kejal, whose frown vanished.

Kejal then broke into a smile and walked toward Hawk and put his arm around him.

Hawk looked over his shoulder at Jaziri. "Does he know I don't understand the Sorani dialect? I only know Kurmanji."

Jaziri laughed and waved dismissively. "You'll figure it out." He turned and walked back toward his truck before driving away.

For the next hour, Hawk trekked the hills with Kejal. Hawk wasn't surprised that a man who spent his entire work week herding goats would be so talkative. Despite their difference in dialects, Hawk understood the gist of Kejal's long-winded stories. Kejal once served for Saddam Hussein in the Iraqi National Guard, a fact he was proud of. Since it was disbanded, he'd returned to his family's business of herding goats but had used his military training on several occasions. Kejal related a story of how he once disarmed an ISIS militant while making a routine visit to his bank in Rawanduz. It sounded somewhat fanciful to Hawk, who wasn't sure if either he didn't quite understand the dialect as much as he thought he did, or if Kejal was simply engaging in the time-honored tradition of embellishment. Language barrier aside, Hawk won over Kejal by following social cues, laughing when he laughed and giving a look of empathy when he looked pained. It was critical to gain Kejal's trust.

When Kejal finished telling his latest story, Hawk asked if Kejal minded if Hawk walked across the terrace and check out the other side of the mountain. Kejal agreed but told Hawk he'd have to go alone since the terrain was too dangerous for the goats.

Perfect.

Hawk hiked toward the edge and identified the coordinates from the note he'd found between Karif Fazil and Moradi. He pulled out his binoculars and studied the compound located atop another terrace. Strategically, Fazil couldn't have picked a better location in the area. Several nearby caves could provide cover—or entrapment—during an attack. There were several ways to get up to the compound, but all of them required four-wheel drive vehicles to navigate the steep embankment.

While Moradi might have had something personal against Fazil, he would've never been able to mount any type of retribution against him there. Moradi's specialty was IEDs, not hand-held missile launchers. The only viable way to attack the compound would be through the air. But Hawk had time. The most important element of his overall mission was to eliminate Nasim Ghazi. Without Ghazi in the picture, Al Hasib wouldn't be able to generate the type of devastation their weapons expert had wreaked on U.S. interests over the past few months. But was Ghazi even there?

Hawk glanced back over his shoulder toward Kejal and waved. Kejal smiled and waved back.

Peering through binoculars, Hawk saw something that made him sick to his stomach. Peeling his eyes away, he looked off in the distance and strained to hear a faint noise. He looked through the binoculars again and focused them.

And then all at once his worst fear was confirmed as he looked skyward.

CHAPTER 8

KARIF FAZIL STROKED his pet pigeon, Jafar, which stood perched on his shoulder, and looked out over the canyon below. He felt like a king surveying his dominion. In the distance, waterfalls gushed forth into the canyon. Birds soared overhead. The slight breeze easing across the deck of the residence quarters atop his compound was the only sound—other than that of the voice nagging him non-stop in his head.

Attaining the kind of power he wielded wasn't accomplished through polite diplomacy. It was something he had to want—something he had to take. And more often than not, it required ruthless action to acquire it. People in the west talked about burning bridges as if such an act were a bad thing. For Fazil, it was necessary to keep his enemies from coming after him.

He grabbed a pinch of grain from his seed bag and held it out for Jafar. The pigeon vigorously pecked at it, snatching up one grain at a time with its beak.

"Good girl," Fazil said as he rubbed Jafar's head with his index finger.

Fazil was waiting on a shipment of IEDs. He'd struck a deal with a middleman, a local opium supplier, who was instructed to purchase a large cache of IEDs from Rasul Moradi. If it weren't for the fact that he got caught having his way with Moradi's younger sister, Fazil would have worked directly with Moradi and avoided the markup. But Fazil could afford the extra cost, especially since it also offered the added protection of making the transaction more difficult to track for the local Iraqi authorities who refused to take one of his generous bribes.

The IEDs would be deployed to distract people from the real target. As a student of war theories, Fazil had become enamored with Germany's Schlieffen Plan from World War I. Had it been executed properly, many German generals believed it would have led to German success in the war. Fazil concluded that creating two war fronts as the aggressor was a blueprint for success rather than defending two fronts. He wanted to dictate the terms to his enemies, something he was gearing up to do in two days.

The real target—the front Fazil was more interested in fighting—would get hit when no one suspected it. While every security force would be concerned with a rash of IEDs, they wouldn't be expecting the sucker punch he'd deliver. And he couldn't wait to take his swing.

"In two days, Jafar, the world will know about Al Hasib," Fazil said as he stroked his bird again. "Everyone will take note of who we are and what our objectives are."

Fazil would've never dreamed that he would be standing at this precipice—the leader of an international organization committed to overseeing the destruction of Western interests and ideals in the Middle East. If he was honest, he was as an unlikely candidate as anyone could imagine. He'd been educated in the west at Stanford University, studying economics. Before he left for the United States to study there, he always defended American policies with his more militant friends. "Just because we don't agree with American values doesn't mean it doesn't operate as one of the most efficient governments in the world," he told his friends when they questioned his loyalty to their country. "We can take the good and leave the bad."

But Fazil never considered joining the cause of what he considered mad men until that day—that one fateful day.

Fazil received the message on his voicemail that his father had been killed. And though it wasn't quite as painful as watching his mother die as she gave birth to his younger brother, it was far more gut wrenching. Fazil's father was a local farmer who never had any interest in affiliating with the Taliban or any other terrorist group. But a raid by U.S. Marines resulted in his death. They believed several high-level Taliban leaders were hiding out at a local seed store when Fazil's father was there. He was collateral damage, at least according to the final official report issued by the U.S. military. Their apologies and generous check couldn't bring back Fazil's father. So, Fazil took the money and created his own terrorist cell. He was going to strike back at U.S. interests—and hopefully kill a few U.S. citizens along the way. By hitting key targets and developing a marketing team that could've earned him millions the honest way, Fazil put Al Hasib on the map.

"That's right, Jafar, we're going to make them pay a thousand times over for what they've done," he said as he leaned against the deck rail. "A thousand times over."

Fazil's assistant rushed through the door and handed him the phone. "You need to take this."

Fazil answered the phone. "Yes?"

"Everything is in place."

"Excellent. Just wait for my command."

"How soon do you think we'll act? A day or two?"

"Be ready to go within twenty-four hours. I'm

ready to hit them even harder."

Fazil hung up and smiled.

Whoever says vengeance isn't sweet must've never gotten revenge.

He took a deep breath, soaking in the fresh mountain air. He closed his eyes and turned his face toward the sun. It was almost perfect.

Then his peaceful moment was interrupted by a distinct sound, a sound he knew all too well.

He rushed inside and grabbed his binoculars before scanning the horizon.

Fazil gasped and rushed inside. "Drones! Drones!"

He raced down the stairwell, continuing to yell to his fellow warriors.

Less than a minute later, the Al Hasib complex exploded as a pair of drones rained down missiles on it.

CHAPTER 9

SENATOR BLUNT STOOD as he watched the grainy images from the drone's camera while the missile zeroed in on its target. It appeared headed straight for home perched atop a scenic apex in the Zagros Mountains. He would've preferred to witness the destruction of Al Hasib's leader in person, but Firestorm's secret operational command center would have to suffice.

As the drone zoomed closer, Blunt could make out the figures of people sprinting for cover. Then a flash of white and the screen went dark.

Blunt jammed his unlit cigar into his mouth and chewed on it for a few seconds.

"Did we get them all?" Blunt asked.

"Waiting for satellite imagery to confirm, sir," answered one of the officers.

The screen blinked, and a new image appeared. "Can you get me infrared?"

"Gimme just a second," the officer said.

When the infrared image popped up, the cigar nearly fell out of Blunt's mouth, which broke out into a wide grin. "It looks like we got every last one of those cockroaches."

He pumped his fist and sat down in his chair. "We need to spread the news about this. We shouldn't have any problems maintaining funding now."

"Sir, I'd hold off on that until we get confirmation on the ground. We don't know that Fazil was there for sure."

Blunt leaned back and waved off the officer dismissively. "Screw it. There's no way they survived that blast."

The officer sighed. "With all due respect, sir, if we didn't get him, everything you've worked for would be gone, and the budget committee would have all the ammunition they'd need to shut us down."

Blunt took a deep breath and slumped his shoulders. "You're probably right. But I want this confirmed on the ground ASAP."

He exited the command center, almost skipping. He wanted some fresh air and a few minutes to soak in his victory.

No better way to start your morning than killing a few dozen terrorists and securing funding for your black ops division.

He ducked into a nearby coffee shop and bought

a large mocha before returning to his office.

His momentary giddiness vanished when Preston walked into his office with a grim look on his face.

"What's the matter?" Blunt asked. "Did you not get to Madeline Meissner in time?"

Preston shook his head. "We've got far bigger problems than her."

Blunt's eyes widened. "What could be worse than her?"

"For starters, an emboldened Al Hasib."

"What? We just blasted those fools back into the fifth century."

"Apparently, your drone strike didn't get them all, as they took to social media in the aftermath of the attack, bragging about how only a few of their fighters were killed and the majority of the casualties were civilians—and that they have a big surprise attack coming very soon against U.S. interests."

"That's just terrorist bravado. I saw several of their men running for cover when we destroyed their compound in the Zagros Mountains."

"Bravado or not, it's already got Guy Hirschbeck fired up." Preston handed his phone to his boss.

Blunt quickly scrolled through a story that had hit major news media websites with quotes from Hirschbeck about how the U.S. policy in dealing with Middle Eastern terrorists was only proving to exacerbate the problem by creating more terrorists.

He read Hirschbeck's quote aloud: "Every time we strike terrorists with drones and fail, taking the lives of innocent civilians, we incite more hatred for our country, spawning a new generation of people who will stop at nothing to see the downfall of this great nation."

He handed Preston his phone back. "This ought to make our next budget meeting very interesting."

"Well, with all due respect, sir, wasn't the point of Firestorm to reduce the number of drone attacks so what he's talking about doesn't happen?" Preston asked.

Blunt nodded. "The key word there is reduce. Drones can still be valuable when there is a high concentration of high-value targets. That strike today was a perfect example of that."

Preston stared at his phone. "These images of dead children tell a different story."

Blunt rolled his eyes. "They probably found a few kids on the mountainside and killed them and staged their bodies there for a nice propaganda photo opp."

"Regardless, you know you're going to catch a lot of flack for this."

"I'll happily catch any amount of flack from anyone as long as the end result is weeding out these terrorists."

"But isn't that what Brady Hawk is for, to make sure these things don't have to happen?"

Blunt glared at him. "Brady Hawk is for whatever I want him to do. He knew what he was getting himself into. He'll be fine. And if he isn't—well, that's just part of the job." He paused. "By the way, why haven't we heard from him yet?"

CHAPTER 10

ALEX NEEDED SOMETHING STRONGER than breakfast comfort food from The Golden Egg—something much stronger. She hadn't spoken with Hawk since he went dark in the Zagros Mountains. And she couldn't get Blunt to answer her calls after she received a message from a former colleague that some drones targeted a location in western Iraq. She didn't really need confirmation. After working with Blunt for just a short while, she knew he'd bombed those coordinates she'd given him as sure as she was alive. And she hated herself for ever passing them along—even if it was her job.

But at that moment, her primary concern was finding out who Gordon Jefferson was.

She called one of her former colleagues from the CIA to find out if she could help her out.

"I'm not seeing anything in our database on a Gordon Jefferson that would fit the profile of the guy you described," said Mallory Kauffman.

Alex took a deep breath. "Are you sure? I saw his ID."

A moment of silence.

"You still there, Mallory?"

Another long pause. "I am, and you're not going to believe what I just found."

"Lay it on me."

"Apparently, Gordon Jefferson is a legend for an FBI agent named Joel Cochran. Jefferson was involved in an undercover sting to nail an arms dealer from Kazakhstan."

"So, what was he doing talking to me?"

"Beats me. Maybe he knows something—just wanted to see the innocent people out of the way before the FBI swoops in."

"Why would they try to bust Blunt and his special task force? It's the best thing we've got going right now in the way of combatting terrorism."

"I still don't have an answer for you."

Alex listened as Mallory typed furiously on her keyboard. "Are you finding anything else?"

"Nope. Nothing useful anyway. Just a list of Cochran's exemplary service for the FBI."

"And I kicked the crap out of him."

"Alex, you can't beat yourself up for that. You didn't know. I would've done the same thing if some guy approached me like that in a parking garage. In fact, I probably would've done something far worse."

"I didn't have my gun on me."

"I wouldn't have needed a gun."

Alex forced a chuckle before turning serious again. "So, you're sure there's nothing going on that I should know about?"

"I haven't heard any chatter about this anywhere. It's mind boggling, to be honest."

"Okay, thanks. Just send me Cochran's contact information so I can pay him a little visit. I need some answers—fast."

Alex hung up and meandered down the sidewalk until she came to her favorite bar, The Luxe. No matter the time of day or night, the place was full of interesting characters. She could mull her fate in relative peace while she observed the odd couples filling the booth benches. The bartender's mirror was a vital tool in espionage.

With all that was going on, she didn't want anyone watching her or following her. She wanted to be the one doing the watching, the one in charge of any surveillance. And whoever Gordon Jefferson—or Joel Cochran—was, she was going to find out.

Her phone buzzed with a text message from Mallory. It detailed Joel Cochran's address.

She looked at her screen and smiled.

I'm going to have to pay someone a visit—on my terms.

CHAPTER 11

HAWK DIDN'T NEED TO WATCH the dramatic explosions behind him to know what was going on. Alex had passed along the coordinates he gave her, and Blunt had lit up the mountainside. It'd be several days before they could confirm any deaths, though Hawk doubted Fazil was dead. Terrorists were worse than weeds, somehow finding a way to thrive in the most adverse conditions.

He scrambled down the hill and jumped on Kejal's motorcycle.

"What are you doing?" Kejal screamed.

Hawk didn't turn around then either. There was no point in even acknowledging a man who'd been his fellow goat herder just moments before. Not a chance in hell he'd be back in this part of the world, no matter how much Blunt might have begged. The area was scorched earth, thanks to the senator's strategy for dealing with terrorism.

Everything Blunt had done stood in stark

contrast to the very reason Firestorm was created. Hawk was supposed to eliminate such blanket bombing, secretly making terrorists vanish while creating a safe environment for the rest of the world. And it'd worked great.

But Blunt took the first opportunity he got to go after a terrorist without Hawk, strafing a mountainside with his top asset nearby at an undisclosed location. It was reckless and brazen. Perhaps it was what the U.S. needed to win the war on terror, while losing it at the same time. Drone incidents *were* the reason Blunt offered for starting Firestorm. Since then, Blunt had created his own, all because he could. It sickened him.

Hawk tore down the hillside on Kejal's dirt bike and didn't look back. If one member of Al Hasib escaped and identified Hawk, his journey back to civilization would already be more treacherous than it stood to be. As long as Kejal didn't nurse a grudge, Hawk would be fine—that and the two grand he planned to leave with the bike would hopefully be enough to guarantee Kejal's silence.

Hawk didn't stop until he hit Rawanduz. He hid the bike and let Jaziri know its whereabouts. Next, he connected with a former Navy Seal colleague who was working in private security there. Hawk abided by some steadfast principles in his operations, chief among them the idea that you never enter a situation without an escape hatch. Carl Delgado was his escape hatch, the man who could make Hawk disappear if the situation necessitated it. He trained with Delgado, who didn't stay long with the Seals either, but for other reasons.

The next morning Hawk was part of a convoy headed for Kirkuk for supplies, riding shotgun with one his former colleagues.

"How's the good life?" Hawk asked after they cleared the first checkpoint.

Delgado gazed out the window as if he were deep in thought. "You call living in this dust pit where my life is constantly in danger and I'm far away from my friends and family *the good life*? This is more like the gates of hell."

"I thought the money was good."

"Can't spend it on anything out here. We have to smuggle in good booze. It's not like I'm buying a house on a golf course here either. The sooner I can get out of here, the better."

"So, what's keeping you?"

"Hawk, I know you probably don't know about this, but sometimes people make, well, for lack of a better term, rash decisions—decisions they come to regret."

Hawk laughed. "Sarcasm is an art for you, isn't it?"

Delgado cracked a faint smile and continued. "Let's just say I've made my share of regrettable decisions. And unfortunately, I have to pay for some of them."

"Gambling?"

Delgado nodded. "I can barely afford to gamble these days—don't think I would if I could. I've learned my lesson, but it's why I'm still here."

Their truck rumbled along as the tire kicked stray rocks up into the wheel well, creating a cacophony in concert with the hum of the large engine and the whine of the tires on the cracked pavement.

"So, how much longer before you've paid off all your debts?"

"Not much longer. I should be home within a few months, provided I get paid on time."

"Is that a problem?"

"Only when some blood thirsty general decides to bomb a mountainside, forgetting that there's a major pipeline flowing through it. If the oil doesn't flow, the money doesn't either."

"You've gotta believe me when I say that wasn't the plan, and I had no knowledge that was going to happen."

Delgado slapped Hawk in the chest playfully. "Don't worry. I don't blame you. It's those nimrods in Washington who shoulder all the blame. There are just some things..." His words trailed off as he peered down the road.

Hawk strained to see what Delgado was looking at. "What is it?"

"Looks like an impromptu road block."

"Think they're looking for me?"

Delgado shook his head. "Just relax and let me handle this."

The truck came to a stop and a gunman walked up to the driver's side window. Delgado started yelling at the man before climbing out of the truck and confronting him on the ground.

Hawk grew more uneasy the longer the spat continued. One of the other guards eyed him for a few moments before walking over to another guard and whispering in his ear as they both glared at Hawk. Meanwhile, Delgado's animated conversation with the gunman persisted.

"What's going on?" Hawk asked.

Delgado waved Hawk off without even a glance.

He watched in awe as their conversation turned amicable before the man handed Delgado a stack of cash. Delgado climbed back into the cab of the truck and fired up the engine.

"What was that all about?" Hawk asked.

Delgado smiled. "Looks like I won't be here much longer." He thumbed the edge of the bills. He then turned his gaze toward Hawk. "But you will."

Delgado pulled his gun and trained it on Hawk. "Keep your hands in the air."

Hawk realized what he'd just witnessed—a transaction for him.

"How could you?"

Delgado sneered. "Not all of us have Daddy to fall back on and bail us out when we make mistakes. Sometimes you have to be resourceful."

"Or a coward and a back-stabbing fool."

Hawk held his hands in the air in a posture of surrender. "You really think those fools are going to let you out of here."

Delgado shook the money with his free hand. "I'm bettin' on it. Now get out of the truck."

Hawk looked out of his window and saw three gunmen had gathered nearby and were waiting for him.

"You're unbelievable."

"Good luck, Hawk."

Hawk climbed out and slammed the door behind him. Delgado gave Hawk a mocking wave as he rumbled forward along the road. He choked on the dust kicked up by the truck and offered his hands to the men who surrounded him.

Nobody said a word as one of the men zip-tied Hawk's hands behind his back and led him to a jeep a few meters away. Hawk used his elbows on the side of the vehicle to steady himself as he stepped up and inside.

In the back seat, a man settled next to Hawk and aimed his gun at him. He then gestured toward a black box behind them.

"Your father makes great weapons," the man said as he eyed Hawk.

Hawk glanced at the name—Colton Industries—emblazoned on the side of the box. He looked back at the man, who was grinning. It was the last thing Hawk saw before they blindfolded him.

The jeep lurched forward as it started to move, spinning around quickly and returning toward Rawanduz.

"Karif Fazil will be most pleased to see you," the man said.

CHAPTER 12

BLUNT OPENED *THE WASHINGTON POST* and reveled in the headline that the drone strike had been a success. Twelve members of Al Hasib were dead. *Score one for the good guys in the war on terror.* It wasn't quite the good news that he wanted though. Karif Fazil somehow managed to avoid getting killed, not to mention Al Hasib's chief bomb maker survived as well. And children were allegedly killed in the attack. Then there was the matter of a missing Brady Hawk.

It had been more than twenty-four hours since Hawk had last checked in with Alex—longer than that since he'd heard personally from his top asset. When he hired Hawk, there was a risk that he'd go rogue and vanish. If Hawk was ticked over how Blunt handled the Al Hasib complex, he could be upset. Upset enough to disappear? Blunt wasn't sure. But he *was* sure that of all the special agents he'd ever worked with, Hawk had the best chance at going off the grid and never being heard from again.

He kicked his feet up on his desk and leaned back, pondering how he would handle the slew of imminent conflicts that would inevitably arise later that day. He had agreed to a meeting with the reporter Madeline Meissner and would follow that up with a budget committee meeting led by Guy Hirschbeck. His evening would conclude at Nationals Park where he'd watch his beloved Houston Astros get pummeled by the hometown team while meeting with oil industry lobbyists who always wanted more than they were worth politically—or even financially.

Preston knocked on the door and slipped inside after Blunt's acknowledgement.

"Sir, I'm sure if you've looked at your schedule, you know by now that this is a big day for you," Preston said, sliding a folder across the desk.

"Just another day on the Hill," Blunt said as he picked up the folder and opened it.

"I'm afraid it's much more than that."

Blunt's eyebrows shot upward. "Oh?"

"One of my contacts at *The Post* told me last night that Meissner has what she needs to take down Firestorm."

"I'll believe it when I see it. Besides, I have the support of the government and a couple centuries of U.S. foreign policy on my side."

Preston held up his index finger. "I'm afraid

that's not how she sees it, and it might not be how the American people see it."

"I don't care how the American people see it. They have no clue what it takes to keep them safe. I'm one of the few people with the stomach to do what needs to be done. That's why they elected me in the first place."

"To help keep them safe?"

"That and help keep their wallets fat enough that they don't notice what else is going on in the world. If they're paying attention to the Kardashians and not global issues, they'll be happy and keep electing me."

"Meanwhile, you get richer and more powerful."

Blunt put the folder down and glared at Preston. "Just whose side are you on anyway?"

"Just stating the obvious."

"Exactly. There's never a need to state the obvious. Now get outta here so I can get prepared for this pesky little reporter."

"Very well, sir," Preston said before exiting the room.

***

AT HALF PAST TEN, Madeline Meissner was introduced formally to Blunt before he offered her a seat in the small sitting area in the corner of his office.

"Would you like a cup of coffee, Maddie?" Blunt asked. "It is okay if I call you Maddie, isn't it?"

"Miss Meissner will suffice, Senator," she shot back. "And, no, I don't need any more coffee this morning."

"Fair enough," Blunt said as he interlocked his fingers behind his head and leaned back. "So, I'm assuming you want to continue our brief conversation after my speech the other day."

"You'd be correct about that. However, I have a few other things I'd like to cover first."

Blunt shrugged. "Go ahead. It's your show, Maddie."

She sneered at him before looking down at her notes and studying them for a moment. "How effective do you feel the American foreign policy is working in these countries that are harboring terrorists?"

"Our policy has always been to defend American interests, whether at home or on foreign soil. Working in concert with those governments, we've been able to achieve great strides in rooting out the terrorists."

"Now, the drone program has undergone a tremendous amount of scrutiny recently, especially in the wake of the latest strike that killed young children and—"

"You know good and well those bodies were planted there," Blunt snapped. "We're very strategic in those strikes as we've drastically reduced them in recent years. It doesn't take a trained forensic analyst to look at those kids from the pictures Al Hasib disseminated to realize that those kids weren't killed by a missile strike. They were shot, point blank. And most likely by Al Hasib operatives."

"Can you confirm that?"

"I can't comment on specific offensives."

"But isn't that what you just did? It's no secret that your secret program was involved if you have this much intimate knowledge about that attack in the Zagros Mountains."

"I'm not sure where you're getting your information from, but it's severely flawed," he said. "You best be careful what you print for fear that it boomerangs back on you."

"You mean like it did with Nancy Goetter?"

"The journalist who committed suicide by stepping into the path of a moving bus a few weeks ago?"

"She didn't commit suicide. She was pushed."

Blunt shook his head and sighed. "What did nearby security cameras show?"

"Only one had the corner view—and the video somehow vanished, recorded over by someone."

"Happens every day, especially when businesses have to find ways to cut spending with shrinking budgets. This isn't some vast conspiracy, no matter how much you allege it to be."

"You saying it isn't, doesn't make it true."

Enraged, Blunt stood and snatched Meissner's phone off the table in front of her, turning off the recording feature. He slammed it down on the table and glared at her, leaning in close. "Now, I don't know who you think you are, Miss Meissner, but you listen to me and you listen close. You are dabbling in things of which you truly know nothing about. And if you continue to do this, you're putting the security of this country at stake—and I won't allow that to happen."

She gathered up her phone and notebook, stuffing them in her bag. "Are you threatening me, Senator?"

He cracked a faint smile. "I don't make threats— I make promises. And you can ask my constituents. I always keep my word."

"And what does that mean for me?"

"I think you can figure it out. Perhaps you could ask Nancy Goetter."

Her eyes narrowed as she stared him down. "I think we're done here."

Blunt put his hands on his hips. "Don't forget about what I said."

She slammed the door behind her.

***

MEISSNER HUSTLED OUT of the senator's office and didn't stop until she arrived on the steps outside. She reached into her pocket and pulled out her other recording device and turned it off.

She smiled wryly.

Always good to a have a backup.

CHAPTER 13

KARIF FAZIL TOOK A DEEP BREATH and relaxed in the Al Hasib safe house located in the center of Randawuz. His conflicting emotions made it difficult for him to concentrate on the intelligence reports he'd just received from one of his officers. Rage over losing his secret high-tech compound from a drone attack mixed with pride over his foresight to create an escape hatch in case the Americans ever became so emboldened—he wanted to destroy something and celebrate at the same time.

He set down the papers and grinned.

What could be better than celebrating after I destroy something the Americans hold dear?

After all, that was Fazil's mission in a roundabout way. Ultimately, Fazil felt compelled to jihad, a term most Westerners misunderstood to mean acts of terrorism. In fact *jihad* was nothing more than a religious duty all Muslims had to maintain the religion. In the

West, the term became synonymous with holy war, but it was far from that in reality. At least to true Muslims, it meant something different entirely.

Jihad was what his father was doing when U.S. and British forces invaded a school and shot and killed his father. He later learned that it was a school serving as a cover for his father's involvement with a more liberal section loosely affiliated with the Taliban. For Fazil, that only made the pain sting that much more.

Ever since he could remember, his father always spoke about the Taliban in hushed tones, explaining that he didn't agree with their harsh treatment of women. In their part of the world, his father was considered a liberal—even though he rarely discussed it with anyone else. Fazil once found an American magazine hidden beneath his father's bed that was full of pictures of scantily clad women.

When he confronted his father about it, he shrugged. "Allah didn't make woman so we could hide them beneath a tent," he said.

That idea molded Fazil into the paradox that he was today—committed to the Quran, but also progressive in his thinking. How his unorthodox view of Islam manifested itself often caught others off guard, but it also drew in many young people who saw portions of their religion as antiquated and misinterpreted.

"If God didn't want us to enjoy women, why did he make their bodies so beautiful?" Fazil was often quoted as saying. He knew his father must've smiled every time he heard his son repeat more or less what he once said. It was also a popular modern interpretation, one that seemed to be gaining steam within fringe sects of the Islamic community. Fazil concluded that shunning such behavior didn't seem to deter detestable acts such as rape and sexual abuse, so why not embrace the beautiful contours of a woman's body beneath the coverings of bulky burkas? His position wasn't popular with the old guard, but he wasn't interested in a popularity contest. No, Fazil was interested in recruiting new soldiers to carry the banner into war and strike back hard at the Americans. But even more than that, he was interested in revenge.

A knock at the door interrupted his brooding.

"Come in," he said as he continued to stare at the intelligence reports.

"Nasim Ghazi is here to see you," a man said.

Fazil spun around in his chair and laid eyes on his chief bomb maker. He leapt to his feet and rushed over to greet his most important asset in his personal vendetta against the American government.

"Nasim!" he shouted before throwing his arms around Ghazi.

"Karif, my brother," Ghazi answered, holding

the embrace longer than Fazil was used to.

"It's time to strike back for what they did to us," Fazil said.

"Did they destroy it all?"

Fazil nodded. "We haven't been able to get back to the location to confirm it since there are American soldiers throughout the area, but we think so."

"Bastards! We must make them pay!"

Fazil smiled and took a deep breath. "That's exactly what I was counting on you saying." He paused and winked at Ghazi. "Ready to get to work?"

CHAPTER 14

ALEX TOOK A DEEP BREATH and pressed the button next to Joel Cochran's apartment number in the lobby of his modest apartment. After a few seconds, a familiar voice came through the speaker.

"Yes?"

"Joel Cochran?" Alex said.

"Who is this?"

"You paid me a visit the other night, and I want to talk."

A slight pause. "You're finally ready to hear the truth?"

She pressed the button. "I want to listen to what you have to say."

"Very well. Come on up."

Alex ascended four flights of stairs until she reached Cochran's apartment and rapped on his door.

The door opened just a crack, allowing her to see nothing more than an eyeball and a slither of his face.

But she recognized it. For the past day, it was a face that haunted her. Even though she'd managed to subdue him, Alex didn't like the fact that she'd been ambushed by him.

She glanced down and noticed a gun in his hand. "Put the weapon down or I walk."

Cochran sighed and shrugged, appearing to shove the gun into the back of his pants. "Fine—just promise me you'll keep a safe distance." She nodded and he slid the chain lock open. "Come in," he said, gesturing toward the living area as he opened the door.

She stepped cautiously inside, the wooden floor creaking beneath her.

"Please have a seat." He pointed toward the couch. "Can I get you anything to drink?"

She shook her head. "I'm fine, thanks. Hopefully this won't take too long."

He shrugged. "Depends on how much you want to know. I could talk for two days if you'd let me."

"I prefer the CliffsNotes version, please."

They both settled into small couches opposite each other.

"Are you sure?" he asked.

She nodded. "I don't have time for nuance and lengthy background. Just the facts, please."

"It's not that easy."

"Humor me."

Cochran took a deep breath and settled back into his seat. "First, I need to apologize for how I treated you the other night. It wasn't professional, but I felt like I needed to get your attention, and obviously, you found me, like I knew you would."

"You're lucky I didn't break your neck. But I'm a pro at what I do. So, go on."

"There's an investigation going on regarding Blunt and his pet project, and it's not good. Everyone affiliated with it is likely to get blackballed from working with any military group in the future."

She laughed and shook her head. "Already happened with me, which explains why I'm working with Blunt in the first place."

"Well, this isn't like getting the cold shoulder from the CIA—this is like getting thrown behind bars by the feds. What Blunt is doing is illegal, and he knows it, or at least he should. Firestorm is under strict scrutiny right now, and it's going to get shut down. It's just a matter of time."

"So, why me?"

"Firestorm isn't the only black ops program in town."

"A fact I'm very well aware of. And?"

"Well, you're someone who is savvy enough to know what's going on here."

Her eyes narrowed. "You have a position for me?

What, as long as I do the heavy lifting and collect all the dirty laundry on Blunt and Firestorm? Is that what you're hinting at?"

He shrugged. "Dirty laundry or illegal activity—it makes no difference to me how you categorize it. The truth is something needs to be done to put a stop to what's transpiring with Firestorm."

"Oh, now I get what's going on. You've got nothing on Blunt, but somebody wants him shut down. And the only way you can do that is from someone on the inside." She waved at him dismissively. "Well, good luck with that."

"I'm afraid you misunderstand, Miss Duncan. We have the ability to create—how should I say this—uncomfortable pressure points."

She clasped her hands together as her face tightened. "What *you* fail to understand is that the only reason we're involved in Firestorm is because we have no pressure points. We're all luckless losers and loners who can't be intimidated or threatened. As one of my friends likes to say, 'You can't get my goat if I don't have a goat to get'." She stood. "So, if you'll excuse me, I must be going. I can see this was a colossal waste of time, just like your pathetic attempt to intimidate me into betraying an organization full of this country's finest to keeping Americans safe."

"Be careful, Miss Duncan. Not *everyone* in your

organization should be considered part of our finest—and when Blunt goes down, you go down with him."

She strode toward the door before grabbing the handle and stopping. Spinning around, she stared at him. "Better think twice about approaching me again. Next time, I might not feel so generous in how I handle the situation."

Alex exited the apartment, slamming the door behind her. She dug into her purse and fished out her emergency burner phone. Blunt gave it to her when she first started working for him and warned her only to use it when she felt in danger. And while she felt no one was about to sneak up behind her, she certainly felt like someone might be listening, particularly someone like Joel Cochran—whoever he was.

She waited until she reached the street to dial Blunt's number.

"Sir, I think we have a problem," she said as soon as he answered.

"Is it Hawk? Please tell me he didn't get captured."

"I still haven't heard from him, but I'm afraid it's much worse than that."

"What could be worse than losing Hawk?"

"I had a G-man attack me in the parking garage and tell me that *they* were watching Firestorm, and it wouldn't be long before the program would be shut down and everyone involved would be going to prison."

Blunt broke into a hearty laugh. "That'll be the day."

"There's still more."

"Go on."

"I found out his name after I kicked his ass, and then I paid him a visit to find out what was really going down. The truth was whoever he was working for has nothing on us, and they were fishing for someone to feed them information."

"I hope you told him where to stick it."

"More or less—but it doesn't change the fact that someone is coming after us."

"They'll rue the day." Blunt grunted. "Who was the guy who attacked you?"

"Joel Cochran. Works undercover for the FBI. You ever heard of him?"

"No, but I'll take care of him."

CHAPTER 15

HAWK SQUINTED AND TURNED his head to the side as the jeep rumbled along the dirt road. Ever since they'd turned off what sounded like a shoddy cement road, the dust had begun to choke him. He coughed, gasping for a clean breath. It was an exercise in futility.

He felt the end of a gun barrel pressed hard into his lower back. "Don't worry. Not much longer now," the guard said before he broke out into laughter.

Hawk thought about how much fun it would be to snap the man's neck and put an end to his mocking. If Hawk had felt so inclined, he could've done it in the moment. But he was far more interested in learning about Fazil and Al Hasib. If they were going to drive him straight to one of their secret compounds, he was content to enjoy the ride. Ever since they'd left the scene of his betrayal, he'd been keeping track of every movement, guesstimating the distance with each turn and change in speed. Even with the blindfold, he was confident he'd be able to identify the compound where he was headed. The fact that they kept him conscious while they transported him showed either an extreme level of arrogance or naïveté. Hawk didn't care what it was. Either way, they were going to regret it.

In less than a half hour, they arrived at their final destination. One of the guards led Hawk out of the jeep, steadying Hawk by holding him up.

Hawk cocked his head to one side in an attempt to get a feel for the environment. The relative lack of noise led him to believe that it wasn't a compound bustling with activity. It was subdued, perhaps by the fact that they'd lost several comrades earlier in the day thanks to some American drones. Whatever the reason, it didn't seem like a staging area for a high-powered terrorist organization.

Following the lead of the guard, Hawk shuffled along in darkness. He was led inside a building before the door clanked shut behind him. The ground beneath Hawk's feet turned from gritty sand to hard concrete. After walking through several more doors, the guard shoved Hawk into a seat in what seemed like a smaller room. Hawk's suspicions were confirmed when the guard removed Hawk's blindfold and exited through a door behind him.

Hawk surveyed his surroundings, his first opportunity to glance at his environment since he arrived in the compound. Stark concrete walls enveloped him, a lone gray door behind him providing the only exit. He studied the plastic blue chair he sat in, something that reminded him of a seat from an elementary school. But this one was weathered, faded through time. How it ended up in a terrorist compound was probably an interesting story in its own right. But Hawk focused on what he could, the tangible reality facing him. If he was going to escape the compound, he needed to process everything he could—as quickly as possible.

Without the use of his hands, there was only one option left available. He'd use it judiciously, but when the opportunity presented itself, he'd have to act fast.

After waiting in silence for several moments, the door finally clicked open behind him. Hawk looked over his shoulder to see a man accompanied by two guards.

"So, this is the infamous Brady Hawk?" said the man who was obviously in charge.

Hawk was surprised at Fazil's stature, which was much shorter than Hawk expected. At best, Fazil was five-foot, seven-inches tall. Nothing to be scared of. His wiry frame did little in the way of presenting a commanding presence. But when he spoke, it was evident that he was in charge.

"Cut him free," Fazil said.

One of the guards rushed toward Hawk and slid a sharp blade through the zip tie that held his hands together.

Hawk rubbed his wrists and took a deep breath, the first opportunity he'd had to do either since he was traded by Delgado. "Some kind of welcoming party," Hawk said.

Fazil smirked. "You should see what I do to my enemies."

"So, we're *friends*?" Hawk asked, raising his eyebrows.

Fazil snickered. "I'm not sure I've ever treated a friend like this, but perhaps we will be—despite the fact that your government just tried to obliterate me."

Hawk turned his head to one side and flashed a smile. "I'm sure it was nothing personal."

Fazil placed his hands behind his back and circled Hawk. "Perhaps this is all a big misunderstanding, as you Americans like to put it. But I'm not so sure."

"What do you want with me?"

Fazil shrugged. "An apology? Propaganda? An opportunity to show the world that we're stronger than we've been given credit for? I don't know. There are many reasons I could give you."

Hawk took a deep breath and studied Fazil. His

captor had a solid command of the English language due to his extensive time in the U.S. studying at the University of California at Berkley. His eyes turned down, almost sad. And his hair carried a hint of gray to it, already betraying him in his late 20s.

"I'm far more interested in the truth," Hawk finally said.

"The truth?" Fazil said, nodding. "Fine. I'll give you the truth. We're going to make a video of you getting your head chopped off. It'll be fantastic propaganda for Al Hasib." He paused. "Is that what you want to hear?"

"Only if it's the truth."

"Lies are the devil's tools," Fazil said.

Hawk chuckled. "If you only knew how that sounded?"

"What? Do you dare mock me?"

Before Hawk could answer, he began convulsing. His body shook as he twisted and turned, leaning back in his chair and crashing onto the hard floor. Hawk could sense Fazil's presence. If Hawk could read Fazil's thoughts, Hawk knew it'd be something like, "Don't die yet—I need him alive."

"Guards, quick!" Fazil shouted.

Hawk continued to shake violently on the ground, twisting and turning.

"Guards!"

Several seconds later, two guards hoisted Hawk onto their shoulders and carried him out of the room.

Hawk didn't stop his charade the entire time they carried him across the compound. He needed to know what he was up against the second he subdued them and avoided capture. If he was going to survive, he needed to know everything he was up against.

As he glanced around between convulsions, he suppressed a smile.

Hawk liked what he saw.

CHAPTER 16

SENATOR BLUNT LUMBERED into the defense budget meeting and sat down at the head of the table. The room was relatively quiet other than the shuffling of papers or the clicking of thumbs hammering away text messages on cell phones. Blunt surveyed the room and took a deep breath, confident that his pet budget projects would pass.

"Someone looks chipper today," Guy Hirschbeck said.

Blunt rolled his eyes and gave him a dismissive wave. "Your pop gun isn't going to work against this tank. I think this week has already proven my point about why we do what we do."

"We'll see about that," Hirschbeck said.

Blunt's cell phone buzzed with a text message from Preston: "Call me ASAP". He shoved the phone back in his pocket and turned his attention to Hirschbeck, who called the meeting to order.

"Gentlemen, this meeting should be rather brief. The budget oversight committee has decided that we need to strike only $150 million from the defense committee's proposed budget," Hirschbeck began. "We'd prefer that you not trim anything out of the budget from the military. In other words, this needs to be removed from special projects."

"For goodness sake, Guy, why don't you just challenge me to a duel?" Blunt said.

Hirschbeck's eyes narrowed. "You'd like that, wouldn't you?"

"Did you not see the latest security briefing? A dozen members of Al Hasib were taken out thanks to one of our special projects."

"I'm not here to influence your decision," Hirschbeck said as he leaned back in his chair, placing his hands behind his head. "You make your case among your colleagues. I'm just here to let you know what needs to be done."

Blunt grunted and shook his head. "So, it's just a coincidence that Project Z here has a budget of $150 million? You're unbelievable."

Hirschbeck leaned forward and slapped the table. His eyed widened as he cocked his head to one side. "Maybe it's a conspiracy."

"It's not a conspiracy," Blunt said as he slammed his fist on the table. "It's a damn vendetta."

Hirschbeck stood and collected his papers. "If you gentlemen will excuse me, I'll let you hash this out amongst yourselves and report back to the committee on what you decide. You have until the end of today."

Blunt watched his nemesis stride across the floor and exit the room. He waited until the door shut before he spoke.

"This is a bunch of bullshit if you ask me," he said. "I hope every one of you understands the importance of Project Z and what it means to our national security."

Glenda James, the young senator from New York, held up her hand. "I think I can speak for the rest of this committee when I say that we have no idea what this special project of yours is comprised of. And I dare say that it certainly appears like a conflict of interest for you to be a part of it."

"With all due respect, there's a conflict of interest for each and every person in here on every project, if that's how you want to look at things," Blunt said. "But not with mine. There is no *conflict*—only my *interest* in securing the safety of this great nation."

She held up her index finger. "It's simply a project you oversee with no outside oversight. That's quite a bit of money to have at your discretion."

"Well, Senator James, just look at the results. No international incidents, yet we have—most recently—

eliminated a dozen high-level Al Hasib agents."

"And what of Karif Fazil?" she snapped. "Was he among the dead?"

"We haven't been able to confirm that yet, but we do have agents on the ground investigating."

She crossed her arms and let out a long sigh. "You make it all sound so rosy—yet not a single person here can verify what you're saying."

Blunt shrugged. "The secrecy of this program is what makes it so successful."

"Very well then. We have one other program that could stand to face some trimming, and that's our missile defense program, which is still in development. Several members on the committee have spoken with me about this already, and I think that's what this committee's decision will come down to."

Blunt stood. "Fine. You know where I stand. Not sure that I need to do any more convincing at this point. You know where to count my vote." He collected his papers and stuffed them in his briefcase before turning toward the door. He stopped and spun around. "I hope you know what you're doing, Senator James. The nation's security is at stake. We're all a little bit safer this morning because of this project."

She nodded. "We'll take that under advisement."

He walked confidently out of the room and shut the door behind him. He let out a sigh before heading directly toward a bench in the hallway. He sat down and called Preston.

"What's so urgent?" Blunt asked.

"I just got a call from one of my contacts at Metro PD," Preston said. "They're reopening the case of Nancy Goetter in light of some new evidence that has come to light."

"What new evidence?"

"He wasn't sure, but this can't be good."

Blunt let out a string of expletives, drawing the attention of a woman nearby who glared at him while she covered her young daughter's ears. "I'll be in the office soon."

He hung up, and then his phone buzzed again with a text message from Madeline Meissner.

> **I just received a report from one of my contacts in Iraq that those supposed Al Hasib agents who were killed were locals guarding the compound. The children, however, were indeed killed by the drone strike. Care to comment?**

Blunt stared at the screen on his phone.

Everything he'd worked for was falling apart, and he could do little to stop it.

CHAPTER 17

KARIF FAZIL PACED outside the makeshift infir-
mary, which reeked of urine and sweat. He conceded
that, in the absence of any women, the sterilization
techniques in the medical unit were far from ideal. Yet,
it wasn't bad enough for him to break his strict rule
forbidding women inside the compound.

He rapped on the door, hoping to get an answer
from the two local doctors he paid handsomely to at-
tend to Al Hasib's needs while staging out of their
base near Ranwanduz. Waiting less than two seconds
and getting no reply, he pounded on the door again.

Another moment later, the door cracked open.
"We stabilized him. Would you like to see?" one of
the doctors asked.

Fazil pushed his way past the doctor and stormed
into the room, stopping at the edge of the bed. He
leaned over Hawk, studying him closely.

Hawk's eyes were closed, face flushed, body

limp—all giving him the appearance of a lifeless man.

"Are you sure he's not dead?" Fazil asked as he felt for a pulse on Hawk's neck.

The other doctor stepped back from Hawk's bed, giving Fazil more room. "No, he's very much alive—just sedated. It appears he had an epileptic fit of some sort."

"And you're certain he's going to be fine?" Fazil asked.

"I'd stake my life on it."

Fazil stroked his chin and pondered for a moment the idea of bringing in another doctor for a third opinion, but there wasn't time. In a worst case scenario, he could subdue the American infidel and carry on with the theatrics after his next planned attack. It'd likely make a big splash in the international media and serve as an additional recruiting tool.

However, Fazil enjoyed the drama in what he did. It explained why he chose to minor in Theater and Performance while earning his Mechanical Engineering degree. He won the lead role of Tevye in Berkeley's production of *Fiddler on the Roof* and soaked up the adulation of his progressive thinking classmates who hailed his ability to ignore several millennia of Muslim-Jewish avarice and embrace his part. But that was Fazil's best performance—convincing everyone who knew him that he didn't care about such things and was a modern man devoid of such prejudices. The fact was he hated every minute of it as he paraded himself around on stage as a member of a group of people he hated more than anything.

For Fazil, the world was indeed his stage, and he wasn't going to miss an opportunity to deliver a stroke of genius that had fallen to him by the way of sheer luck. If he were given the opportunity to script how he would inspire the worthy Muslims to join his cause, he was convinced he wouldn't have been able to conjure up a better idea—literally cut off the head of an American spy and the son of a world-renowned weapons tycoon, cutting off the heads of one of the American military branches in a more figurative sense. It's the only way it could be done. Any other way would seem novice and might as well not be done at all.

But Fazil wasn't one to let opportunity slip through his fingers—he never had before, and he especially wasn't going to now.

He paced around the room once more before coming to a stop in front of the doctor in charge.

"Are you sure he's going to be okay?"

The doctor nodded.

"How much longer before he wakes up?"

"Twenty minutes, a half hour at the most."

A grin spread across Fazil's face. "Excellent." He

turned toward one of the lieutenants flanking him. "Tell the camera crew that we need to be ready to broadcast within the hour, and tell Samil to get ready as well." He winked at the man. "And make sure his sword is *extra* sharp."

CHAPTER 18

ALEX WENT BACK TO HER OFFICE and checked for any messages from Hawk. Nothing. She hadn't seen any calls come through on her encrypted cell phone from him, but she considered the possibility that he was in a difficult position and needed to contact her another way. One of the secure lines into the building was the only other way aside from email, and he'd been dark far longer than she felt comfortable with.

It had been nearly forty-eight hours since she last heard from him, but she tried not to let herself worry. With the lack of chatter coming out of Iraq, she figured he must've been okay and survived the drone strike, if that's where he was. If Al Hasib broadcasted the images of dead children for propaganda, they certainly wouldn't miss a chance to show an image of a dead American spy killed by an American drone—if anything, to mock them. No matter how much she told herself that everything must be okay, she found the silence deafening.

She picked up her phone and called Mallory Kauffman at the CIA.

"Did you find him?" Mallory asked.

"A lot of good it did me," Alex answered.

"What happened?"

Alex sighed. "I uncovered a fishing expedition— probably some vendetta against Blunt. They needed someone to spy on Blunt and turn him in."

"Don't they realize he's doing this under the auspices of the federal government? There's nothing illegal about his black ops program."

"Apparently, someone thinks he has too much power or doesn't like the way he's doing things."

"Well, from what I gather, the program was supposed to reduce drone strikes."

"*Reduce* them, not *eliminate* them," Alex clarified. "Though Blunt was warned by one of our operatives not to use a drone against Al Hasib's hideout in the Iraqi mountains—a directive he ignored."

"It's his prerogative."

"That's why we have operatives like the one I work with. He's a trained assassin who can either slip in and infiltrate their ranks or take out key leaders with sniper shots. Whatever works."

"It might be getting results, but not the kind of

results someone more powerful in Washington wants. All it takes is a fickle leader with a burr in his saddle."

"I *hate* this town," Alex said as she let out a long sigh. "There's a reason why nothing ever gets done around here. Too many insecure men with inflated egos."

"It's like high school all over again."

Alex chuckled. "Don't remind me. Those were four years I'd prefer to strike from my memory."

"Too many guy problems?"

"Among other things." Alex paused and tried to direct the conversation back to the original reason she called. "Look, I need to know more about Joel Cochran. If someone is trying to take down Firestorm, I need to know who it is and let Blunt know so we can stop them."

"Fine. Just give me a second."

Alex listened to Mallory clicking away on her keyboard, interspersed with several confused sounds. "Is everything all right?" she finally asked.

"That's strange," Mallory said. "I can't find anything on Joel Cochran."

"What do you mean you *can't find anything*?"

"I mean, he's gone—wiped out of the system. It's like he never existed."

"How does that happen?"

"I don't know. I've seen records get classified all

of a sudden, sometimes while I'm looking at them. But I've never seen somebody vanish like this."

"I'm guessing you've got no idea who could pull of something like this."

Mallory chuckled. "Well, yeah. The head of the CIA or the President."

Alex listened as her friend pounded away on her keyboard. "Aren't there any breadcrumbs anywhere in the server?"

"I swear, this is starting to make me think I imagined the entire Joel Cochran file."

"But you didn't—did you?"

"No! Of course, I didn't. I know what I saw. I gave you his address, right? It was the same guy who attacked you, right?"

"Yeah, but he's just—*gone*? I wonder why."

"I wonder *who*," Mallory said. "There aren't that many people who could hack the CIA's server and make this file disappear."

"Nobody internally could do it?"

"Hypothetically, you could. But you'd have to have access to the CIA's servers. And it's not like it's just in one location. The CIA mirrors its files to three locations in case of a disaster."

Alex tapped her pencil on her desk for a moment in thought before speaking. "So, what you're saying is that his file would have to be deleted on site in all three of those locations?"

"Exactly. Whoever this is, isn't playing around."

"Oh, great. This is the last thing I need."

"Good thing you're a spy, right?"

Alex sighed. "Right now, I'm not much more than a handler for some black ops program that apparently someone with a ton of power doesn't want me involved with."

"But you *can* figure this out. Just remember your training."

"With your help, maybe."

"Alex, I don't know if I can help you much any more after seeing this. If someone starts poking around and finds out that I was the one who accessed these files, I might get called onto the carpet about it. And that's the last thing either of us want."

"You covered your tracks, right?"

"Don't worry about me. I never implicate myself when going off book. They'll never be able to trace this back to me."

"Good."

"But if they were—" Mallory let her words hang for a moment.

"So, what you're saying is I'm on my own then, right?"

"I might be able to help you in the future. But for now, I need to cool it. Too much activity could draw unnecessary attention to myself."

"Okay. Just let me know if you hear anything. I need to get this sorted out, but I'll do it on my own."

Alex hung up and started to pace around her small office space. She put her hands on her head and let out an exasperated breath.

She wanted to stay at the office and wait for a possible call from Hawk. But she had bigger problems to handle, like the very existence of Firestorm. She grabbed her keys and exited the building.

Alex had to know who Joel Cochran really was, and there was only one way to find out.

***

A HALF HOUR LATER, Alex knocked on the door of Joel Cochran's apartment at the end of the hallway and waited. After several moments, she rapped again on the door. Still nothing.

She looked behind her and knelt down to see if there was any light coming from the apartment. It was all dark. Again, she glanced over her shoulder to make sure no one saw her before picking the lock. Following a few seconds of cajoling, it clicked open. Alex slowly turned the door and walked inside.

"Hello?" she called. "Joel, are you here?"

She waited a second before she turned the lights

on—and gasped.

The room was completely bare.

She rushed outside and checked the number on the door. Fishing her phone out of her pocket, she searched for the text message Mallory had sent with all of Joel Cochran's information. She double-checked the address in the message with the number tacked to the door. It was the same.

Mouth agape, she dialed Mallory's number. She scurried through the apartment, turning on every light in search of some sign that someone hurriedly moved out. If there was a clue, she didn't see it.

Come on, Mallory. Pick up.

"Hi, you've reached Mallory. I can't come to the phone right now. You know what to do at the beep." *Beep.*

Alex hung up and dialed again. This time the call went straight to voicemail.

She shoved the phone in her pocket and headed for the door when she was met by a gruff elderly gentleman.

"Excuse me, Miss, but how did you get in here?" the man asked.

"I—I was in here earlier this evening, and I thought I'd dropped an earring here," she said as she fiddled with her ear.

"That's impossible—unless you broke in earlier this evening."

"What do you mean?"

"Nobody has rented this apartment in over two years."

"It's been vacant *that* long? In *this* housing market?"

He nodded. "So, you mind telling me the truth this time? What are you doing in here?"

"I already told you the truth, Mister."

"I'm afraid that's about as far from the truth as you could possibly get, Miss Duncan."

Alex glanced at the man and decided to make a run for it. And she almost made it. But he firmly grabbed the back collar of her shirt, whipping her head back as her body lurched forward.

The man slammed her head into the wall and watched her body crumple to the floor.

CHAPTER 19

DURING ALL THE COMMOTION, Hawk figured he could sneak a peek as he feigned consciousness during his fit. Fortunately, he'd seen enough before one of the doctors had jammed a needle into his arm and knocked him out.

When he regained consciousness, he was careful not to move. He surprisingly didn't feel any restraints on his arms or legs. It was a far better situation than he imagined. Using his auditory senses, he listened to the ambient noise in the room. His best guess was there were no more than two people watching him. If they were armed or not was simply information he couldn't yet gather. With two people hovering about him, he had to assume that they were waiting for him to awaken.

He heard the door open and a familiar voice speak in a language he understood. "Is he awake yet?" the man asked.

"It won't be much longer," came another voice. "I'll let you know the moment he wakes up."

Hawk heard the footfalls in the hallway grow fainter and fainter. After they all but disappeared, he heard the two men speaking softly to one another.

Here goes nothin'.

He cracked his eyelids just enough to see the room and scanned it. A small square window in the far corner provided all the light, but it was sufficient even on a cloudy day. In the corner were two men enjoying what appeared to be two cups of tea. One wore a side arm over his shoulder, while the other appeared to be a doctor of some sort with a stethoscope slung around his neck. The room contained medical equipment, including a blood pressure machine and a heart monitor. An oxygen tank sat in the corner of the room along with a machine gun.

Perfect.

Hawk's eyes darted back toward the two men, who continued to converse in the corner. He slowly moved his arms to make sure he was indeed untied. But just as he was about to make his move, he decided to wait as a piece of their conversation arrested his attention. He strained to make out all the details—the words "bomb" along with "Doha" and "Ritz Carlton" were enough. It wasn't perfect intel, but it'd suffice under the current conditions. And it was time to go.

In one smooth motion, Hawk leaped off the table, catching both men by surprise. He grabbed the back of their heads and slammed them together, knocking the doctor out and dazing the soldier. Hawk finished him off with two swift uppercuts before snatching the man's handgun and ripping his machine gun off his body.

He slung the machine gun over his shoulder and grabbed the oxygen tank. Peering through the slightly opaque window pane, Hawk could see enough to recognize he was on the second floor of the building he'd scoped out while faking his seizure. Presenting another challenge was the lack of a handle to wrench the window open and climb through. He dashed over to the door and cracked it to see a pair of guards at the end of the hall. Fortunately, he'd been quiet enough to avoid drawing their attention, but their presence made drawing unnecessary attention too soon quite problematic. He weighed his options and decided his best plan of attack would be to go out through the window.

Hawk, who borrowed the soldier's keffiyeh, hoisted the oxygen tank over his head and smashed the window. Doing his best prairie dog impersonation, he popped his head up quickly and glanced out into the common area to see if he'd attracted much attention. One soldier looked in his direction, but he waved him off dismissively as if to say everything was fine. The soldier shrugged and walked away.

He surveyed the area and identified an unmanned jeep with a machine gun mounted on top. The jeep was idling a few meters to his left at the base of the building.

Hawk grinned. *That's my ride.*

He then threw the oxygen tank out of the window, heaving it in front of the jeep and toward the center of the common area. Undaunted by the small shards of glass still in the window frame that dug into his skin, Hawk slithered through the opening and jumped down toward the ground. The same guard, who didn't seem too bothered by the broken glass a moment before, took a keen interest then and rushed toward Hawk's position and began yelling.

Hawk aimed his handgun at the oxygen tank and shot it, ending any dream of a stealthy getaway and replacing it with a sure-fire chaotic escape.

A layer of white smoke hovered just off the ground, creating a frenzy among the Al Hasib soldiers. Gunshots ripped through the air. Guards screamed. Meanwhile, Hawk covered up his face and drove right through the smoke and toward the compound exit.

The gate was only partially open, but it was more than enough for Hawk. Slamming his foot on the gas, he downshifted the jeep and barreled toward the opening. Once the two guards at the gate realized what was happening, they began shooting at Hawk. He ducked and continued to plow through the gate and down the dirt lane leading to the main road.

Bullets whizzed past him, several striking the jeep. Hawk slumped down in his seat as much as possible and continued driving. In his rearview mirror, he could see that he'd attracted two initial pursuit vehicles with more certain to follow. He took one hand off the steering wheel and reached back with the other, stretching just far enough to finger the trigger on the machine gun mounted atop his vehicle. He waited until he was clear of any possible collateral damage to other vehicles before he squeezed off a few shots, spraying the roadway behind him. The two vehicles—one jeep and another modified pickup truck—swerved back and forth but maintained their pursuit.

As the Al Hasib soldiers continued to shoot, Hawk identified a turnoff ahead with a world of possibilities when it came to ridding himself of at least one of the vehicles. Just off the main road was a dirt road that dipped into a rocky canyon. Hawk pulled hard on the steering wheel, catching both vehicles off guard by what he saw in the rearview mirror. He zoomed down the road, creating a suffocating cloud of dust.

Hawk ripped past several rural homes where

goats and chickens roamed freely. More than a couple of men shouted at him with a raised fist. Eyeing the vehicles behind him, they managed to keep pace and peppered his jeep with an occasional round of gunfire.

Darting up and down hills, Hawk finally saw his opportunity. Up ahead was a cliff, blocked off by a flimsy wooden barrier. With all the dust his jeep was kicking up, he played a hunch that they didn't know about the looming dropoff. Up ahead and to the left was a craggy mountainside that would have to suffice for his jump.

Hawk slowed down his jeep just enough to let them get close but not so close that they'd notice the sign. He then stomped on the gas and counted.

Three ... two ... one ...

He threw the jeep into neutral and jumped out with about a second before the vehicle reached the barrier. Slamming into the rock face hard, he grabbed a pair of hand holds and looked over his shoulder in time to see the two vehicles soar off the cliff after his vehicle. Once they cleared the cliff, he wandered near the edge to see how far they'd fallen. All three vehicles hadn't stopped tumbling and flipping down the steep embankment.

Hawk let out a sigh of relief. He'd done nothing more than buy himself some time. If he thought it was challenging to get out of Rawanduz before, it was going to be a near impossible feat now—especially without a vehicle.

He turned around and saw a boy gawking. Hawk caught himself gawking as well but not at the boy. He was staring at the kid's motorcycle.

"How much?" Hawk asked in his best Sorani as he pointed at the bike.

The boy scowled, acting as if he was insulted by the suggestion.

"How much?" Hawk asked again, wondering if the boy didn't understand.

"It's not for sale," he said.

Hawk dug into his shoe and pulled out his emergency money. He was careful not to pull it all out. He glanced down at what he'd fished out. "Fifteen hundred U.S. dollars? Is that enough?"

The boy's face lit up. Hawk knew it was enough to buy three beat-up motorcycles plus put plenty of food on the boy's family's table for several months.

Without delay, the boy rushed over and snatched the money from Hawk's hands. "She's yours," he said.

Hawk smiled and nodded in appreciation. He wasted no time in spinning the bike around and tearing back down the same route he'd come.

Once he reached the main road, he headed toward town in search of a pay phone. He had to let

Alex know what he'd heard about the bomb at the Ritz Carlton in Doha. Without the benefit of knowing when it would happen, Hawk realized it was unreliable intel, but at the very least it might save a few hundred lives if due diligence was enacted at the hotel.

After he found a pay phone, Hawk parked his bike and followed protocol. He couldn't call Alex's cell phone since he didn't have a secure line. And he didn't have one on the landline either, but his time was dwindling, and he'd have to take a chance.

Hawk dialed her number and prayed she answered. Voicemail.

"Where are you?" Hawk said. "I need to speak to you urgently. I'm alive, but there's a code red going on. A bomb has been planted—or will be planted—at the Ritz-Carlton in Doha."

He resigned himself to the fact that he'd have to try later to share any other extraneous details he picked up. But how much later, he didn't know. Not with Al Hasib agents hunting him, and him being a few hundred miles away from safety.

Hawk stared down the street and sighed. This assignment was testing all his skills, forcing him to harken back to his training. Nothing was going to be easy.

A man tapped him on the shoulder, and Hawk spun around.

"Are you Brady Hawk?" the man asked.

Hawk eyed him closely. "Who are you?"

"I'm a friend. You need to come with me right now before you wind up dead on the street."

Hawk went against his training and followed the man, saying another short prayer under his breath.

CHAPTER 20

INSTEAD OF STAYING AWAKE to hear the results of the committee's final vote, Blunt decided to go home and drink until he fell asleep or passed out—whichever came first. It made no difference to him. Just get the day over with and maybe the next. He'd enjoyed controlling everything for a few months and hoped for more, but it appeared as if all the characters in his life were about to control him—quite possibly for a long time.

He awoke to a throbbing headache and a cold bed. For the past several years, he'd been used to both. It's what happened when a woman walks in on her husband with his scantily clad twenty-something assistant going over more than just the next day's schedule. Blunt managed to weather that storm with his constituents as well, calling it another way his foes tried to distract the voting public from his stellar record. While Blunt would've preferred to take credit for that line, Preston was the one who created such a masterful spin that Blunt won re-election by the biggest margin he'd ever had during his tenure.

After he got out of the shower, his phone buzzed on the bathroom counter. It was the only man he'd answer the phone in the nude for.

"Mornin', Preston," Blunt grumbled.

"Good morning, indeed, sir," Preston replied in a chipper voice. "I assume you saw the results of the committee's vote from last night?"

Blunt grunted. "I already have a hangover to start my day—I'm not a sadist."

"Then you'll want to hear this—Firestorm is still on. In fact, they increased fifty million to two hundred million dollars."

"Who got the shaft?"

"James. She had a pet project pegged at two hundred million for upstate New York for some worthless testing facility that one of the other committee members pointed out. Poof. It's now gone forever."

Blunt wiped the mirror and for a moment stared at himself, mouth agape. "You've gotta be kidding me."

"Nope. And it gets even better."

"Better?" His voice rose another octave.

"Yeah. A little birdie delivered an email last night to *The Washington Post* editor with proof of a little plagiarizing that some reporter on his staff had done."

"Madeline?"

Preston chuckled. "Yep. Before her editor had an opportunity to properly investigate those claims, a few other organizations got the tip, too. And now she's no longer employed by *The Post*."

Blunt rubbed his hands together. "Is it December 25th?"

"Well, there's still the little hiccup of Metro reopening the Nancy Goetter case."

"I trust that won't be a problem, will it?"

"Absolutely not. I'm already working on it."

"Excellent," Blunt said. "You know, Preston, I think my headache is gone."

"If I could only bottle my magic and sell it to others—"

Blunt broke into a hearty laugh. "I'm a greedy bastard, Preston, and I need all that magic for myself. You got that? Don't be spreadin' this around to anyone else."

"See you in the office, sir."

Blunt hung up and whistled a cheerful tune as he started getting dressed.

With fifty million more dollars, I can have a whole company of Hawks. We'll pound those terrorists back into the sand.

The thought of Hawk jogged his memory that

he still hadn't heard from his top agent in the field. No doubt his decision to call in a drone attack on the Al Hasib base was not popular with Hawk. But Blunt didn't imagine it would send him off the grid—not for so long. Three days was twice as long as he'd ever gone without hearing from Hawk.

Blunt could handle getting chewed up by the press, but the idea that Hawk might be harboring a grudge was unbearable. Ever since Tom Colton first made a sizable donation to Blunt's campaign, he had been going over to Colton's house and mingling with him and his family.

On Hawk's tenth birthday, Blunt attended a dove shoot that Colton held for several political power brokers on his land in east Texas. Blunt brought Hawk a baseball signed by Nolan Ryan and a special playoff football signed by Emmitt Smith.

"For me?" Hawk said as he stared slack-jawed at the gifts.

Blunt nodded and smiled, tousling Hawk's hair.

"Thanks!" Hawk said as he continued to stare at his new prized possession. Then he looked up after a moment. "Can I call you Uncle J.D.?"

Blunt swelled with pride since he and Carolyn didn't have any kids of their own at the time and not a single nephew. "Of course you can. Call me whatever you like."

"I think Uncle J.D. suits you best," the young boy said before scrambling upstairs to his bedroom.

Though they'd had their share of run-ins over the years, Blunt was always confident that Hawk wouldn't forget their special bond. It's why, as happy as Blunt was over Preston's Problems-Be-Gone Elixir, Blunt still had a nagging feeling that something wasn't right with Hawk.

Blunt picked up his phone and called Alex, hoping that she could give him an update. As the phone rang, he remembered that she told him she'd call him the second she heard something. And she'd be uncharacteristically silent.

When she didn't answer, he called the man who was supposedly running Firestorm.

"General Johnson speaking," the man answered.

"This is Blunt. Have you seen Alex Duncan lately?"

"She's been in and out lately, but she's been here."

"Has she made contact yet with Hawk?"

"Not to my knowledge, sir, but you know I'm not always privy to some of the more sensitive missions you coordinate with them."

"I know that can be irksome sometimes, but it's how we protect ourselves."

"Yes, sir. I understand."

Blunt sighed. "Very well. The minute you see her,

would you please ask her to give me a call. I have something important I need to discuss with her."

"I'll make it happen," Johnson said before hanging up.

Blunt sat back down on the end of his bed and rubbed the back of his neck with his left hand. Firestorm had only three agents in the field, but his best one was missing. He felt his headache returning.

CHAPTER 21

FAZIL PEERED OVER THE CLIFF above the smoldering wreckage caused by Brady Hawk. It was disheartening enough that the American had escaped and killed several good soldiers in the process. But what angered Fazil the most was the fact that the second Al Hasib compound in a few days had been compromised. He suspected they might have two hours tops before the Americans unleashed another drone attack. An immediate evacuation needed to commence—something he didn't have time for as he prepared an attack that would demand the world's attention.

He kicked at the ground near the edge, sending a spray of rocks and sand into the cavern below. Frightened, Jafar fluttered in the air for a few moments before alighting back onto Fazil's shoulder. Turning toward one of his lieutenants, Fazil snapped his fingers. "Send a team of men down there to get their bodies. They're all heroes, and we must celebrate them as such."

He strode back toward his jeep and climbed into the passenger side. With all that was going on, he'd forgotten he was supposed to talk with Nasim Ghazi to ensure that everything was running smoothly. He pulled out his phone and dialed Ghazi's number.

"Is everything ready?" Fazil asked.

"I'm walking to the hotel right now."

"Excellent. Wait for my mark."

He hung up and suppressed a smile. With such a big victory so close for Al Hasib, it was cause to celebrate. But he learned long ago that a triumph wasn't so until it was.

During the fledgling years of Al Hasib, Fazil and Ghazi were working on a plot to blow up an international boarding school in Abu Dhabi. They'd identified six high-profile public figures from the U.S. and Europe who sent their children there. And since it was far easier for them to penetrate the school's security than it was to attack a dignitary shielded by multiple layers of protection, they opted for the plan that had a higher chance of success. Yet the mere conception of the plan would've been almost impossible without Ghazi's vast array of skills.

While Fazil positioned himself as the mastermind of the group, he conceded—only to himself—that Ghazi was the only reason Al Hasib hadn't remained a feckless terror organization. On the surface, it seemed like a perfect match, but in truth, it was a union borne out of both happenstance and intentional plotting.

Nasim Ghazi wasn't his given name; he was born Carl Edward Butler. As he grew up in a neighborhood full of Muslim immigrants in New York, he began to develop enmity toward his classmates at school who viewed their U.S. nationality as superior to any of his international friends. For years, he never acted on the rage welling within him, choosing instead to do something to stop it.

When Butler graduated from high school, he attended college and obtained a mechanical engineering degree to appease his parents. But as soon as he tossed his cap and ditched his gown, Butler applied to the police academy. He was promptly accepted and emerged as a detective-specialist for the New York City Police Department's Bomb Squad.

During his two years on the force, Butler disarmed and disposed of more than two dozen bombs, the majority of which were set by Muslim terrorists. Sometimes he dismantled them before anyone in the general public found out about it—other times they were high profile cases that were covered by national media. However, given his position, he often crafted the narrative that it wasn't a bomb created by Muslim extremists but by some other domestic terrorist group. He falsified reports to reflect that it was someone else other than who investigators initially suspected. He wanted Americans to understand that terrorists were everywhere, even living among them. More than that, he wanted the average American to understand that just because they didn't look the same or even speak the same language, didn't mean they were a threat to the American way of life. Over time, he began to see what a fruitless endeavor he'd embarked upon.

Meanwhile, he began to secretly meet with some of those terrorists through his Muslim friends, urging them to stop. They politely declined, insisting that it was the only way to make their voices heard as they struck back at the American crusaders who sought to destroy their way of life. Though Butler didn't agree with them at first, as he developed relationships with them, his mind slowly changed. He joined a local mosque and grew a beard. At work, he endured endless teasing, especially when he announced he was legally changing his name to Nasim Ghazi.

One night, not long after he went out with his fellow officers to a local bar, Butler refused to drink, citing his new religious beliefs. However, he saw it as an opportunity to explain to his co-workers about what it meant to be Muslim and how they should be more sensitive to those living among them who weren't as homogenous. In closing, he made an impassioned plea for them to stop their snide comments and hateful attitudes. In hindsight, Butler admitted that he should've chosen a time when they might be more receptive—a time that didn't include alcohol. Though the only reason he was willing to admit as much was due to the severe beating he received that night. For ten minutes, his officers punched and kicked him.

"You think you're better than us?" one of them yelled before delivering a swift kick to his thigh.

"You think Islam is the religion of peace?" another asked as he punched Butler in the head.

After they stopped, Butler rolled over in the alleyway, unable to get up. Fifteen minutes later, an elderly man wearing a yarmulke stopped and helped him up.

"I never thought I'd get help from a Jewish man," Butler said as he regained his balance.

The man smiled at him and patted him on the back. "Sometimes you have to leave where you are to have the life that you want. Perhaps by choice or not."

Butler watched the man shuffle away down the sidewalk. He packed up his belongings that night and bought a ticket to Afghanistan.

And Nasim Ghazi was born anew.

Ghazi took the old man's advice and started over

in the Middle East. But he wasn't about to let go of his desire to strike back at the arrogant Americans.

When he arrived in Afghanistan, he asked around about a young man named Karif Fazil. Ghazi had heard a report from the BBC that during an attack by allied forces, they'd killed several innocent civilians, including a man with a son named Karif Fazil. Fazil was interviewed for the report—and his words haunted Ghazi.

"My father was doing his job and making a delivery from his butcher shop when American soldiers stormed in and shot him," Fazil said as he started to sob. "How can it be that these men can come into our country and shoot an innocent man? How can it be that these men can come into our country and take away my father?"

And from the moment the two men met, they embarked on a venture that bonded them together—to strike back at the Americans who'd dared to set foot in their part of the world.

While they'd struck hard and fast at American tourist destinations in the Middle East and American interests, the failure at the school in Abu Dhabi always stuck with Fazil. They'd managed to sneak into the school and plant nearly four hundred kilograms of C-4 explosives throughout the building. Once they retreated outside, they hid in a wooded area nearby and prepared to detonate the bombs and watch the grand explosion. Fazil and Ghazi smiled at one another, but when they pressed the button, nothing happened.

They panicked, checking and rechecking the detonator. Only later after it was revealed publicly that a terrorist plot had been thwarted did they learn that the school was equipped with a radio-jamming device to prevent such attacks. The pain of such a failure always reminded Fazil to temper his excitement.

He rode back to the compound and instructed everyone to grab as many weapons as possible and evacuate the premises. The last truck was leaving when his phone rang with a call from Ghazi.

"Is everything all right?" Fazil asked.

"It's fine. Are you ready?"

"Do it."

"Good. I also thought you might want to listen to this as it happened, perhaps my atonement for the school in Abu Ghazi."

"You've atoned for that a hundred times over. Now, let's hear it."

"It'll be my pleasure," Ghazi said before he pressed the detonator.

The grin Fazil had worked so hard to suppress erupted on his face as he listened to the explosions followed by shrieks and screams. Jafar cooed as Fazil nuzzled his face against the bird.

"Well done, Nasim. Well done."

CHAPTER 22

ALEX'S HEAD WHIPPED BACK in the direction of the mystery man with such force that she lost her footing and fell flat on her back. But she wasn't about to surrender so easily. She rolled over only to be greeted by the point of the man's boot against the side of her face. As she clambered to her feet, Alex was almost upright when the man attempted a roundhouse kick, but this time she was ready.

Alex grabbed the man's leg and twisted it, flipping him over. She kicked him in the face and rolled him over before placing her arms around his neck.

"Who are you?" she said.

The man didn't answer, instead choosing to struggle out of Alex's grip. He failed to break free, his face paying a heavy price as she pounded him several more times in the head.

Finally, the man collapsed.

Alex grabbed her phone and took the man's fingerprint with it. She forwarded it to Mallory and then dialed her.

"Do you ever sleep?" Mallory asked as she answered the phone.

"Look, I don't have time to get into everything right now, but I just sent you a fingerprint. Can you look it up for me?"

"Did you kick some guy's ass again?"

"I didn't have a date tonight."

Mallory snickered. "You really need to get a personal life. It might help with all that pent up frustration you apparently have."

"Just doing my job."

"Do you remember the part where I told you I needed to cool it for a while so I didn't attract unnecessary attention?"

Alex ignored her question. "You found it yet?"

"Geez, give me a second. I need to start the search first. So, while we're waiting, do you want to tell me what happened?"

"I went back to Cochran's apartment, and it was completely empty."

"Already?"

"Yeah. This guy posing as the landlord said it had been vacant for a couple of years."

"So you beat him into submission?"

"Pretty much."

"I'm so glad you're my friend," Mallory said. Her

computer beeped. "Okay, let's see what we got here."

"What is it?"

"Oh, great. It's classified. I'm gonna have to answer a bunch of questions in the office tomorrow about this."

"So, nothing?"

"Yeah, nothing it is. Whoever he is, he's got a protected status, and I can't get access to his file. But I might be able to do some digging."

"Fine. Let me know what you come up with."

"I suggest you get out of there, Alex. There are some pretty dark ops groups he could belong to, and they wouldn't appreciate you handling one of their agents like that."

"Roger that. I'm out. I'll look for your call."

Alex hung up and proceeded to rifle through the man's pockets. Nothing. No cell phone. No gun. Not so much as a pack of chewing gum. She took a picture of him and exited the apartment.

Once Alex reached the street, she walked for a block toward her car. She couldn't shake the feeling that she was being followed. Nonchalantly, she peeked over her shoulder to see if she was being followed but didn't see anyone. She turned the corner and glanced behind her once more before letting out a sigh of relief.

That's when she felt a firm grip take hold of the back of her arm.

She gasped and was spun around to see Joel Cochran.

"Joel," she said. "You scared me."

"I hope so," he said. "You shouldn't be hanging around here. I've already warned you once."

Her eyes narrowed. "Who do you work for?"

"You wouldn't believe me if I told you."

"Try me."

"Honestly, it's not that important. But what is important is that you get out of here before you get yourself hurt—or worse."

"Joel—or whatever your name is—your apartment was cleaned out when I just went back there to get some answers."

"What do you want to know?"

"I want to know what's really going on."

"I've already told you. If you don't believe me, that's your prerogative. But you've been warned."

"Who are you working for?"

"Alex, asking me more questions isn't going to get you any more answers. You just need to trust me and bail out." He handed her a card. "This is how you can reach me if you change your mind. Just don't get caught working for Blunt. It's not going to be pleasant for him in the coming weeks."

She shoved the card into her pocket and glared at him. "I know I'm helping keep our country safe, but I've got no idea what you're doing. So, don't expect to hear from me."

"Suit yourself, but I tried to help." With that, Cochran spun and walked away.

Alex watched him and wondered what was happening, unsure who to trust. She walked for another block and got into her car. She looked at her phone and realized she had a missed call from an unknown number.

That had to be Hawk!

She called her office phone and heard his message, alerting her to the developing situation in Doha.

She shoved her key into the ignition and turned it. The car roared to life. She put the car into drive but froze when the radio came on with a special report.

"More than a hundred are dead and fifty more injured in a well-planned terrorist attack on the Ritz-Carlton Hotel in Doha, Qatar, today," said the man on the radio. "However, officials expect the death toll to rise over in the coming hours. Al Hasib is claiming responsibility for the attack."

She was already too late.

Reluctantly, she picked up the phone and called Blunt. Based on his grumpy disposition, she figured he'd either been asleep or was drinking.

"About time you called," he said once he picked up his phone.

"I finally heard from Hawk."

"Is he okay?"

"I'm not sure. I just got a voicemail from him, warning me about Doha."

"Doha? What's happening there?"

"What *happened* there," she said. "I'm surprised you hadn't been called already."

"What *happened*?"

"Al Hasib. The Ritz-Carlton in Doha—gone. Around a hundred dead and more expected."

Blunt grunted. "So, where's Hawk?"

"He didn't leave me a forwarding address or any clues for that matter. I'll just have to wait for him to reach out again."

Blunt didn't speak for a moment.

"Is everything all right, sir?" she asked.

"No. No, it's not! My best agent is missing, and I don't know where the hell you've been over the past couple of days. No one knows where you've been or what you've been up to. If you'd been at your desk, perhaps you could've prevented this massacre in Doha."

Alex sighed. She didn't want to tell Blunt what he wanted to know. "I'll find him, sir. Don't worry."

"You better," he snapped and then hung up.

Alex stared at the screen on her phone. Perhaps Joel Cochran was right—life was about to get very difficult for Senator Blunt. And that's not something she wanted to be around for. Or perhaps there was something else more sinister at play.

She couldn't decide what to do and wished someone would tell her which direction to go.

Then her phone buzzed again. It was Mallory.

"You're not gonna believe this," Mallory said.

"I doubt anything will surprise me at this point."

"I hacked into the database and found out whose fingerprint this belongs to."

"And?"

"Harry Bozeman."

Alex sighed. "Am I supposed to know who that is?"

"No, but you'll know who he works for."

"And that is?"

"A secret task force run by none other than Senator Blunt's favorite person, according to you—Guy Hirschbeck."

CHAPTER 23

AS HAWK FOLLOWED the man down a back alley-way, he contemplated running. After all, it wasn't too late to leave the guy. He was starting to second guess his instincts and question whether sheer desperation had clouded his judgment that much. The thought was fleeting, and he continued behind the man.

After several turns, the man jammed a key into a lock and opened the door, gesturing for Hawk to enter first. Hawk complied but turned his body sideways so he could keep an eye on what was inside as well as on the man.

The man chuckled. "Don't worry, Mr. Hawk. I'm not going to hurt you." He slapped Hawk on the shoulder and pushed past him toward a common living area.

Hawk stopped and scanned the room along with the surrounding area.

"Can I get you some tea?" the man asked as he set his jacket down over the arm of a chair.

"That'd be nice. Thanks. You Brits can't go six hours without the stuff, can you?"

A few moments later, the man emerged from the kitchen adjacent to the living area. He pointed toward a chair on the opposite side of the room. "What can I say? We do love our tea. Now, please, have a seat."

"How do you know my name? And what's this all about?" Hawk asked, still bewildered by the fact that the man knew his name.

The man sat down and crossed one leg over the other. "The *how* and *why* are interesting questions, for sure. However, the real question that needs to be answered is *why*."

"As in, *why me?*" Hawk asked, pointing at himself.

The man shrugged and then nodded. "Something like that."

"So?" Hawk said, his eyes widening. "Go on."

"Many years ago, your father asked me to look out for you so that's what I'm doing."

"My father made you my personal guardian angel of the Middle East? Isn't that special?" Hawk said as he laughed nervously. "I never knew he actually cared about me that much. I only thought he cared about himself."

The man cocked his head to one side. "Your father is a far better man than you think. Besides, I'm neither a therapist nor an apologist for your father. I'm simply here to do what he asked me to do."

"And *what* exactly is that?"

"To make sure that you succeed at your mission."

"How would you or my father know about my mission—or even care, for that matter? I don't even know your name."

"My apologies," the man said as he stood and offered Hawk his hand. "Eric Angel."

Hawk shook the man's hand, and a faint smile crept across his lips. "When I said you were a guardian angel, I—"

Angel waved Hawk off and chuckled. "I get that all the time—so much so that I'm considering using a code name in the future."

"Why? Eric *Angel* doesn't even sound believable."

"Well, I can assure you that it is real, though you won't find me in any of your CIA databases."

"I don't work for the CIA, Mr. Angel."

"I know. You work for Senator Blunt, but that's close enough. You get my drift."

"You're a ghost."

"Some people might say that, but you can see me sitting in front of you, right?"

"Plain as day."

"Very well then. Let's get to the business at hand."

Hawk shifted in his chair. "Which is *what* exactly?"

"Helping you catch Nasim Ghazi."

"What makes you think I need your help?" Hawk said.

"Perhaps the fact that I was embedded with Al Hasib for two years."

Hawk sat up in his seat. "*You*? *You* were embedded with Al Hasib?"

"A most unpleasant experience, I can assure you. But it's true."

Angel cocked his head to one side. "And you know what they're going to do next?"

"Not exactly, but I do know some of their *potential* targets, none of which bode well for U.S. interests."

"Care to enlighten me on which ones that would be?"

"They won't move fast after the bombing in Doha. They'll want to let what Al Hasib did fester."

"Blunt wants me to take out Nasim Ghazi."

"I highly recommend that. Without Ghazi, Fazil will be left in a lurch. My personal observation is that Ghazi is the real brains behind the operation."

"So, you think there might be a power struggle brewing within Al Hasib?"

Angel shrugged. "Perhaps. But regardless of what Fazil might want to do next, he would be a fool to attempt anything without Ghazi's help. Ghazi's thoughtful planning—and special bomb-making skills is what has empowered Al Hasib to garner international attention."

"And what's your interest in seeing him stopped?"

"Like I said, I'm only fulfilling a promise I made to your father years ago to look out for you and ensure your success as an agent."

Hawk closed his eyes and shook his head. "He doesn't think I'll amount to much, does he?"

"Quite the contrary," Angel said. "He believes you're going to be an agent who changes the world—you just need a nudge in the right direction."

"How come no one else has taken out Ghazi? And why do you think I'm the one to do it?"

Angel stroked his beard for a moment and leaned forward. "Others have tried to take him out and obviously failed." He pointed at Hawk and continued. "But it'd be a fool's errand to send anyone else to do the job. He's a savvy guy and smells trouble right away. But *you*? You just might be able to penetrate Al Hasib's inner circle enough to get a shot at him."

"Like I said before, why me?"

"Because you've got the intangibles to succeed?"

"Such as?"

The man got up and retrieved the tea kettle that was whistling. He returned moments later with a cup for Hawk. He held it up. "Because you have people skills, especially in this part of the world."

"What has that got to do with anything?"

"That's your ticket in," the man said with a smile.

"Come again."

Angel took a sip of his tea and then sat back in his chair. "While Ghazi bounces around from place to place in the Middle East, we just recently learned where he's truly based out of—Zaranj, Afghanistan. It's on the border near Iran and is virtually ignored by the U.S. forces in the country. And it's where he'll go when he returns to hiding."

"He won't be with Fazil and the rest of Al Hasib?"

"Fazil has at least a dozen hideouts and compounds, and he has no discernible pattern as to where he goes. He prefers that his top lieutenants remain at large and only assemble when necessary to make it more difficult to cripple the group should they get hit by a strike."

"So, I'm supposed to just go into Zaranj and use my people skills to gain their trust and win them over?"

"Something like that. I'm sure your handler will think of something appropriate for you. But it's the best way to get access to Ghazi. However, you best not delay. This window of opportunity won't last long."

"Let me talk with my superiors about this." Hawk stood. "I can't make decisions unilaterally on the field."

"Whatever you do, make it quick. If Ghazi disappears again, who knows how many people he'll kill."

Hawk nodded and offered his hand to the man. "Thank you."

"No. Thank *you*. It's an honor to meet you after all these years." He paused. "I trust you'll take these words to heart."

"Don't you worry, Mr. Angel. I'll make sure that we capture Ghazi and cut off the head of the snake. I'll make you proud."

Angel smiled. "You'll make your dad proud, too."

Hawk set his tea cup down and hustled toward the door.

"Wait," Angel said. "Before you go, I need to ask you to do something for me—something very important."

CHAPTER 24

BLUNT AWOKE THE NEXT MORNING to the sound of his doorbell. He pulled the covers off and stumbled toward the door, tying his bathrobe around him as he went. He peeked through the hole and shook his head in disbelief.

I'm gonna kill her.

"Get in here, Alex," he said as he opened the door and snatched her inside. He shut the door behind him and leaned against it before he started to tear into her. "What do you think you're doing coming here to my house in broad daylight? You have no idea who might be watching me—or you. That's the kind of carelessness that gets agents killed or compromised or both."

"I'm sorry, Senator. It's just that I found out something else that you need to know, something very important."

The scowl vanished from Blunt's face. "Did you speak with Hawk?"

She put both her hands up. "No, not yet. This has nothing to do with him."

"While I still think you jeopardized everything by coming here, information about Hawk and his whereabouts are about the only thing worth risking your cover for." He gestured toward the door. "So whatever this is, I'm sure it can wait."

"I'm afraid you'll have a different perspective once I tell you what's going on."

He crossed his arms and glared at her. "Go on, and make it quick."

Alex proceeded to tell him about why she more or less went dark on him and some of the people she met in the process. Then she dropped her bombshell.

"I had a friend of mine at the CIA do some digging into who the mystery man was that ambushed me in the apartment that was fully furnished just a few hours before. Turns out he works for another special classified project run by none other than Guy Hirschbeck."

Blunt furrowed his brow. "That makes no sense. Why would Hirschbeck be in charge of some secret project? He's been on the Hill just long enough to figure out where the restrooms are and can *still* barely wipe his own ass."

"Don't get mad at me—I'm just the messenger here." She held her finger in the air. "But it might explain some of his animosity toward you. Perhaps he thinks you're stepping on his toes."

"I'd stomp on them with steel-toed boots if I could find his feet, believe me when I say that."

Alex nodded as if she understood.

Blunt started to pace around the entryway. "We've got to be extra careful from now on. While I wish I could say this surprises me, it doesn't. This is Washington politics and government bureaucracy run amok as usual. Some pencil-neck geek has a personal vendetta against me for who knows what reason, and he's weaseled his way into creating some secret task force to suss out information about what I'm doing. He's either overly curious or overtly dangerous. Either way, we have to be careful that he doesn't learn about Firestorm."

"Who all knows about what we're doing?"

"Not many people, but the President himself is the one who requested that I lead this thing. If I had my druthers, I'd be in the Caribbean with some attractive woman and drinking Jack and Coke about right now. But nobody tells the President no."

"Would it save everyone a big headache if you looped him in?"

"Look, Alex, there are plenty of things I appreciate about you—your tenacity, your willingness to get the job done even if it means bending the rules a little.

I have no doubt that might come back to bite me one day, but I'm willing to live with it because you're the right person to be working with Hawk on this team. And while I appreciate your optimism, it's sprinkled with far too much idealism. In case you haven't figured it out yet, the main reason Firestorm is so secretive is because it's illegal, more or less. We're operating far outside the boundaries of what's permissible under the law. And you can bet there's enough hacks on the Hill who'd love to write an expose on Firestorm, and even more political foes who'd love to pin this on the President and try to put him behind bars. So, I—"

"Just stop right there," Alex said. "I know about all this; it's just that I thought there might be an easier solution."

"No solutions are easy in Washington. Everybody has to get their fingers in the pie, whether for their constituency or their legacy. And while I'd love to take Hirschbeck out somehow, it'd come back to haunt me, I'm sure."

"Fine. I'll let you handle it your way."

Blunt's eyes locked with Alex's. "You better. It'll be more than your job at stake if you dare to confront Hirschbeck. I'll take care of it. You and Hawk just go kill some terrorists, okay?"

She nodded. "I'll let you know after I speak with Hawk."

"Good. I don't care when it is, give me a call, but don't come over again like this."

He opened the door for her, and she left. He locked it behind her and shuffled toward the den.

After brewing a pot of coffee, Blunt settled into his favorite easy chair and watched the morning news. He could hardly concentrate after what he did to Alex.

He didn't hate lying, but he hated lying to her.

CHAPTER 25

TWO DAYS AFTER THE BOMBING, Fazil took a quick trip to Kabul to visit his mother. The guilt he shouldered for leaving her gnawed at him, but he assuaged it by sending her plenty of money. She refused to spend any of it for a long time, questioning where it came from. He dismissed her concerns by telling her that his American education served him well, and that he was a wealthy investment broker who traveled extensively. She eventually came to believe him and decided that it would be acceptable for her to spend the money.

With Fazil's guidance, she purchased a home on a ridge overlooking Kabul. It was a sprawling mansion that came with a cook, a gardener, and a security detail. While its grandeur was striking, she had told Fazil on many occasions that she'd trade it all to have her husband back.

However, Fazil had ulterior motives for getting his mother to buy this particular house. For starters, it was a gated community. And aside from the main entrance, it was virtually impenetrable since the back half of the house overlooked a craggy canyon. Even savvy rock climbers might think twice about attempting to scale the face of the wall.

But there was also a hidden room beneath the house that Fazil's mother didn't even know about. With a secret entrance along the side of the house, Fazil and his colleagues could access it without being seen and without raising the suspicion of Fazil's mother.

After he finished having tea with her, he told her he had some business to take care of and needed to talk on the phone outside on the veranda. He asked her to watch Jafar for a little while before he slipped around the side and into his secret lair. Inside, he found Nasim Ghazi waiting for him.

"Brother," Fazil said as he greeted Ghazi with a hug and a kiss. "It's been far too long."

"No doubt about that," Ghazi said as he released Fazil from the embrace. "We have much to talk about."

"And we have much to celebrate. Your work in Doha was exquisite—not to mention that your image has yet to be captured on any of the security cameras from the hotel."

Ghazi smiled. "That's why I put a few extra

pounds of explosive near the security room to make sure anything in that room is unrecoverable."

"Does anything get past you?"

"In New York, we call that attention to detail."

"Call it whatever you like—it's all the same to me. As long as we strike back at the heart of those infidels."

"Speaking of the infidels, what do you have in mind next?"

Fazil unraveled his keffiyeh. "I was going to ask you the same thing, just to make sure we were on the same page. You know we do this all the time."

"Okay, I'll play along." Ghazi picked up a piece of paper off Fazil's desk and ripped it in half and slapped a pencil on top. "Let's write it down at the same time and see if we're thinking along the same lines."

They each scribbled down a name and folded up their respective sheets of paper.

Ghazi offered his paper to Fazil. "We'll open our papers at the same time. On three—one … two … three!"

They both stared at each other, slack-jawed and amazed.

"Every time," Fazil said. "Allah must be smiling upon us."

"He'll be smiling even more if we succeed on this mission."

Fazil rubbed his face and sighed. "So, what do you think? A week or two?"

Ghazi's eyes widened. "You'd have better luck with a suicide bomber if you want to move that soon, and you won't get near the number of infidels if you took your time."

"So, how much time do you need? A month?"

"Try two at the least. This is a big target. I'll need to spend a couple of weeks scouting out the area and establishing a protocol for how I can gain access and plant the bombs before I return to Zaranj and build the bombs."

Fazil shrugged. "Two months it is. Now pack your bags. We don't have any time to lose. Bahrain awaits."

CHAPTER 26

ALEX DRUMMED HER FINGERS on her desk as she hummed along to Steely Dan's "Don't Take Me Alive" playing through her earbuds. She didn't have many fond memories of her father since most of them were tainted by having to watch him murder her mother. But she remembered watching him cover this song at a dive bar when she was maybe nine or ten years old. His face never lit up like it did that night on stage. Perhaps it was the defiant nature of the song that brought him unusual joy. Alex couldn't be sure. But she was sure she felt defiant right then, especially given the suspicious thoughts that nearly overtook her mind.

Guy Hirschbeck was up to something and so was some other black ops group. And maybe Senator Blunt was as well. It was all such a convoluted mess that she began to wonder what she'd gotten herself into. Maybe being damaged goods wasn't such a bad thing.

I can just go start over in some small town somewhere, teach school, coach volleyball.

The fleeting thought made her happy and momentarily forget just how complicated her life was—not to mention that her job was to serve as Brady Hawk's handler, and she hadn't spoken with him in nearly a week.

The phone on her desk rang, snapping her out of her funk. She yanked her earbuds out and answered.

"This is Duncan," she said.

"Alex—it's me, Hawk," he replied. "I've been trying to reach you."

"I know. And unfortunately, it was too late for us to thwart Al Hasib's plot in Doha."

"If at first you don't succeed—"

"Do you have another lead?"

"I think so. But I need a legend because I'll need to go deep cover."

"Give me the details so I can go over them with Blunt."

Hawk proceeded to share what he learned regarding Al Hasib's protocol and how Nasim Ghazi would be hidden in Zaranj, Afghanistan, building his bombs for their next big attack.

"So are you all right?" she asked. "What happened?"

"Aside from nearly getting my head chopped off

by Karif Fazil's minions only to have to survive a harrowing chase through unfamiliar terrain, things are good. You can read all about it in my report. What about with you?"

"Oh, the usual. Blunt's made more enemies and is in danger of the entire program getting shut down only to suddenly gain more funding. Meanwhile, I was nearly abducted in a parking garage until I escaped and then had to fight my way out against some guy who'd trapped me and claimed to be from some other shadowy government organization."

"Or as I like to call it, the weekend."

Alex forced a nervous laugh. "This is not what I signed up for."

"Someone wise once told me that it never is, and it's called life."

"Touché. Let me get this information over to Blunt and see what he wants me to do. It may take a few hours."

"I'll call back in three."

***

THREE HOURS LATER, Alex answered her phone with a smooth voice. In the interim, she'd gone over the details with Blunt and developed a new legend for Hawk—all of which Blunt approved.

"You're now Simon Wells, a member of the Peace Corps teaching English in Zaranj," she told Hawk.

Hawk didn't say anything for a moment before he sighed. "Really? The Peace Corps?"

"Do you have a problem with that?"

"Have you read my file?"

"Cover to cov—" Alex stopped herself. She hadn't even considered how painful it might be for Hawk to engage in an undercover operation as a member of the Peace Corps. "I'm sorry. I'd forgotten about that."

"Don't worry about it. I'll manage. It's probably the easiest way in on such short notice anyway."

"Hawk, if I could fix it, I would."

"I understand. There's not much time, and you were just doing your job."

Alex paused for a moment before responding. "If you ever want to talk about it, I'll listen."

"Thanks. I might take you up on that one day."

"I'll forward the details to your email account, but I suggest you start making your way there now. I've got you starting in three days."

She hung up and tried to forget about how she'd bungled the move. As much as Hawk insisted it wouldn't be a problem, she wasn't so sure. Using the Peace Corps was indeed the fastest way into the country, but utilizing such a familiar experience—one that was full of pain—could cause problems for Hawk.

More troubling was the fact that it could jeopardize the operation, and that was something she just couldn't live with. But it was too late to do anything about it.

CHAPTER 27

SINCE HAWK EXITED his adolescent years, he could only remember crying twice in his adult life. That's why the tear streaking down his face caught him off guard as he hung up the phone with Alex. While he worked hard to suppress the emotions surrounding his final day in the Peace Corps, he prided himself on the fact that he'd put it behind him. It was in the past—gone forever. Just like Emily Thornton—gone forever.

With Eric Angel's help, Hawk secured transportation to Zaranj in a semi-truck full of goats. It was the least glamorous way to travel, but its contents guaranteed it wouldn't garner more than a passing glance at the border.

Hawk settled into his position in the trailer, as far as he could sit forward. Surrounded by creatures who found joy wallowing around in mud all day, he wondered if he could ever be so carefree in life again. The pain he'd already experienced was enough to break a normal man. But he wasn't normal—at least that's what everyone had told him his whole life. In fact, he was extraordinary, a warrior. Nothing could intimidate him.

In a moment of honesty, he realized everyone had been lying to him. Sure, he might have appeared like that person on the outside, but deep down he craved intimacy and friendship. The kind of relationship he had with Emily.

As the truck bumped along, Hawk had little to do but think and reflect. He pulled the photo he'd lifted off his attacker in Kirkuk and stared at it, wondering who was behind the attempt on his life. But he also couldn't stop thinking about *her*.

But Hawk couldn't think about *her* without thinking about *him*—the man who was responsible for his life but was never really there for him: his father, Thomas J. Colton.

To describe Hawk's childhood as difficult would qualify as both equal parts true and false. He was born to Alicia Elizabeth Hawk, a woman who did the best a single mother could do in terms of caring for her child. Before her son was born, she struggled to make ends meet, aspiring to one day become a teacher. But such lofty dreams required an education, a higher education—an education her alcoholic father and waitress mother couldn't afford. She sought alternate means to pay for her education, working as a stripper for eighteen months to save up money for college. Degrading herself in front of leering men wasn't how she wanted to pay for school, but it was the only job she could get that kept her from living paycheck to paycheck. The money was good, really good. She met with a friend who'd graduated several years ahead of her and had become a teacher. In a month, her friend made half the money she did by just working four straight Monday through Thursday shifts, which were the slowest tip nights. She could make twice that simply by working Friday and Saturday nights. And while Alicia was tempted to forego school, she didn't want to give up her on dream to become a teacher—nor could she see herself stripping for the rest of her life. At some point, she'd have to turn elsewhere for an occupation.

Alicia was set to quit stripping in one week when she met a man who propositioned her outside the club. She told him that she wasn't that kind of girl, but he could take her out to dinner and see how things went. So, he did. But it wasn't just dinner. It was far more. And she never even got his name.

Not that Alicia thought much about it at the time. She quit her job and enrolled in a local community college. But she didn't last long—not because of the academics, but because she couldn't sit in a class longer than thirty minutes without having to get up and puke her guts out. She went to the school's triage and learned that she was pregnant.

"Are you sure?" a teary-eyed Alicia asked the nurse.

The nurse handed her the pregnancy test. "Honey, these things don't lie. You've been knocked up."

Alicia cried all the way home, unsure of what her future held. She weighed all her options but decided to keep the baby. After lecturing her father for years about how he had to accept the consequences for his actions—even when he was drunk—she couldn't be a two-faced hypocrite.

When Braden Christopher Hawk was born, Alicia was a proud mother. But she was also a poor one. Returning to work as a stripper, she struggled to find someone to take care of her little Brady. Her babysitters never lasted long, especially as Brady grew older. He was a strong-willed kid who'd test the limits of anyone watching him. After Alicia missed several consecutive shifts because of her inability to find a suitable caretaker, she plopped down on the couch and turned on the television. She resigned herself to the fact that her life would never amount to much. Then she saw him—Thomas J. Colton, the head of Colton Industries. She realized that he was the man she'd met that night outside of the club.

In a desperate move, she disguised herself and waited in the lobby for him one day. She *accidentally* ran into him, pricking him with a knife. She apologized and volunteered to help dress the wound she'd just created. Irritated, he let her while she savvily scooped up some of his blood. Later that day, she paid a lab a couple hundred dollars for a paternity test. Colton was the father.

She immediately contacted a lawyer and drew up a paternity suit. Colton quickly settled with her for two million dollars with the condition of anonymity. She agreed.

However, when Hawk was fifteen years old and asking questions about his father, Alicia dismissed them as not a big deal.

"I'm the only family you've got, Brady," she said. "And that's all that matters."

It wasn't all that mattered to Hawk. The fact that his mother was independently wealthy yet was working her way through school raised his curiosity. He dug through her file labeled "important papers" one night when she was in class and pulled out the lawsuit. After a quick Internet search, Hawk found Colton's home address and paid him a visit.

At first, Colton's face went pale. He stammered and tried to make excuses—until Hawk whipped out the paternity test confirmation. Colton then invited Hawk into the house. He'd since divorced his wife and decided he owed it to the kid to give him an explanation. But instead of it being a one-time meeting, Colton—who never had any kids while he was married—thought it might be fun to embrace Hawk instead of shunning him. Colton's subsequent influence was what led Hawk to apply to become a Navy Seal and enter one of the most rigorous training programs in the U.S. military. But it only took one mission for Hawk to realize the Seals weren't for him. The mere thought of what he had to do on that mission made him queasy weeks later. Consequently, that single mission was all it took to turn him against the military, and led him to a place where he decided the Peace Corps was a far more worthy way to spend his days as a young adult.

And it was during his thirty-month stint in the Peace Corps that he met Emily Thornton and fell in love with her—then lost her forever.

The truck screeched as it came to a slow halt, the compression brakes unleashing a blast of air skyward. The Iranian military circled the truck at the border stop for a few moments before waving the truck through.

Hawk had almost a day and a half ride ahead of him as the route explained to him by the driver was to cut through the heart of Iran before dropping him in Zaranj just inside the eastern boundary of Afghanistan. A day and a half to think about anything but Emily.

But he couldn't help but think about her.

After all, she was the reason he decided to return to a life hell-bent on eliminating terrorists, one by one.

CHAPTER 28

BLUNT ONCE ASPIRED to be the President of the United States, an aspiration that died a quick death within two weeks of reaching Washington. When he realized that most every elected official didn't serve their people but well-funded lobbyists, he decided he didn't want to be a bootlicker to anyone. He had his own set of ideas about what a great America looked like, and he endeavored to create it. However, he quickly learned that if you don't lick the right boots, you'll be long forgotten before you ever had a chance to be remembered.

Putting aside his pride, Blunt cozied up to the right power brokers in Washington and found himself amassing an unusual amount of power for a senator his age. Before he knew it, he was pulling all the strings from the shadows, which presented one inescapable problem: he was putting a target on himself. He didn't mind a power-hungry senator making a run at him now and then. Those attacks were easily weathered. But he was putting himself squarely in the crosshairs of the party leaders who sought to push him toward an inevitable run at the Presidency. And that was something he neither wanted nor liked.

Instead of politely declining any such invitations, Blunt decided to draw the ire of the decision makers. He crossed party lines on key votes. He leaked sensitive information to the press about those who wanted to see him attain the party's nomination, and there was no doubt who spilled the secrets. Through a series of calculated moves, he managed to earn the reputation of an attack dog instead of a show dog. Even his affair that ended his marriage—one he was happy to escape—was purposefully orchestrated so he'd get caught. He maneuvered his relationships on the Hill with just enough aplomb to maintain his fellow senators' favor without drawing their support for a run at a higher office. And during the process, he embarked on a journey of self-discovery and learned that at the heart of his hope for America was that it'd be a country safe from terrorists.

Leading Firestorm was a dream come true. He wielded enormous power without much in the way of accountability. And he would squash terrorists in the process. All with an even bigger budget.

When he recruited Alex, he surmised that she was the perfect person for the position. Dedicated, loyal, professional. And if necessary, she'd color outside the lines. It's why he never once worried that she'd find out that there weren't really three globe-trotting terrorist hunters in Firestorm—just one. Hawk was it. The other two were assassins who eliminated his political enemies, working on a per job basis.

Blunt picked up his phone. It was time to put one of his assassins to work again.

CHAPTER 29

NASIM GHAZI TOOK A DEEP BREATH and
soaked in the dusty air of Zaranj with a wide smile on
his face. Every time he came back to work in the border town, it made him wish he never had to leave. It
wasn't home but it felt like what home should be like
in his opinion—comfortable, peaceful, safe, family.
New York was never those things.

A gunshot rang out in the distance, and a pair of
jeeps rumbled by with machine guns affixed to the roll
bars. It wasn't quite the true peace he sought, but he
didn't mind it so much since they were peacekeepers,
and they were on his side.

As he walked along the dusty road, a soccer ball
bounded toward him after an errant pass from a kid's
game nearby flew out of the makeshift dirt field.
Using his right foot, Ghazi spun the ball backward and
chipped it into the air before kicking it back to the
kids. The one boy who'd been sent on the search and
rescue mission for the ball flashed a thumbs-up and a

grin at him. That was Basil, the eight-year-old son of a local baker. On more than one occasion during visits to the bakery, Basil had told him how he wanted to play for the Afghanistan national soccer team and win a World Cup—just one of the many stories Ghazi had learned while living among what he considered his new family. He waved back and kept walking toward his bomb manufacturing hideout.

It's not perfect, but it's paradise to me.

But aside from this slice of the world, Ghazi viewed the rest of the globe—and their people—with malice. If being a Muslim had taught him anything, it was that relationships were important. It also taught him that being a Muslim was superior to all other religions. The infidels were missing out on paradise in this world and the next as they sullied the one he lived in. And there was only one way to deal with them.

He checked over his shoulder as he prepared to unlock his small shop. No one was around. He turned the key and stepped inside, sliding the deadbolt into place after he closed the door.

He stopped and inhaled the scent of C-4 wafting through the air. To the untrained olfactory senses, it smelled like tar or plastic. But Ghazi knew the difference. Too many hours hovering over the explosives to not know the difference. He scanned the room, conducting a quick inventory count to make sure nothing had been taken or moved. It hadn't.

Pulling out his notebook and calculator, Ghazi began to compute just how much C-4 he'd need. His next assignment was by far the biggest—and most challenging—during his stint with Al Hasib. It would require far more explosives than he had on hand along with a deft plan to not only sneak it past border patrols but also into his intended target. The two weeks he spent surveying the object of Al Hasib's most ambitious attack told him as much.

But he needed help, the kind only Raja Tawhid could provide.

CHAPTER 30

HAWK MET HIS CONTACT with the Peace Corps at a local deli the afternoon before his classes were to begin. Frank Culbert wore his pants slightly higher than most people and liked his shirts from a vintage era, circa 1972. He pushed his dark rimmed glasses up on his nose and eyed Hawk closely.

"You don't look like my normal teacher," said Culbert. As head of the program in Zaranj for the past eight years, he had plenty of experience to draw upon.

Hawk flashed a smile. "Is it my age or my good looks?"

Culbert forced a laugh and shook his head. "Never mind." He slid a pile of books across the table toward Hawk. "This is the curriculum for your class. Have you ever taught English before to non-native speakers?"

"Non-native speakers? Who else would I be teaching it to?"

Culbert leaned forward as if he was about to tell

Hawk a secret. "There are plenty of people in the United States who have a weak grasp of the English language, though that's far more challenging." He leaned back. "I always ask because some people who've taught English literature back home think it's going to be the same thing."

"I've taught refugees before," Hawk said, ending Culbert's critique of both rookie Peace Corps members and U.S. citizens whose command of the English language was lacking in his opinion.

"Good. But be aware that everything you do is going to be under a microscope. These kids think that you will represent every person in America and ask you strange questions."

"Such as?"

"They may want to know if you've met Jay-Z or Beyoncé—or if you know Kobe Bryant."

"And here I thought we were exporting capitalism."

Culbert slapped the table. "No, just the worst parts of American culture," he added, indignantly. "The day someone asks me about the Kardashians, I'm quitting and moving to the Amazon jungle or some place where there are no televisions."

Hawk laughed. "I'm glad I'm not the only one who thinks they're a waste of air time."

Culbert didn't smile. "Got any other questions?"

"What about my faith? Can I talk about that?"

"Only if they ask, but I wouldn't volunteer too much information. If you're not careful, they'll have you up at dawn for the Fajr prayers."

"Aren't we all up at that time? Those calls to prayer wake me up every morning."

"You get used to it. Just be careful. This place isn't as radical as most in Afghanistan, but the Taliban still has plenty of influence here, and we don't want any incidents. The Peace Corps has been making heavy inroads here, which go far beyond teaching English. And while English was one of the pre-requisites the Afghan government put on us in order to be here, what we're doing in the way of teaching people new farming techniques and adapting to new technology is changing people's lives. It's important work. Don't screw it up by trying to get too chummy with your students—especially the female variety."

"Message received," Hawk said. He stood. "I appreciate your advice and candor."

"If you screw up, I'll be there to tell you about it, along with a ticket for your trip home."

"Understood," Hawk said.

Hawk stooped over, gathered his books, and headed back toward his apartment. He peered back over his shoulder at Culbert, who seemed preoccupied and stared off into the distance.

After his initial encounter with Culbert, Hawk wasn't sure what to make of his Peace Corps supervisor. During his first stint of service with the organization, he noted two things. The first was how idealistic all the young people were who'd signed up to join. The second was how jaded and cynical the elder leaders of the group were. It seemed like a cruel meat grinder: in goes optimism, out comes pessimism. Or perhaps it was just people who'd attained a more realistic perspective on the world by living outside the bounds of the United States. Either way, the final product generally consisted of bitterness or disappointment—or both.

But Culbert? He was hard to read. It was apparent to Hawk that he wanted to come across as a hard ass, but he wasn't so sure if that's who he really was. And he wasn't sure if he would end up being a friend or a liability. He needed to gather some more information, but it was time to hit the books. He had a class to prepare for.

CHAPTER 31

SENATOR BLUNT SPILLED COFFEE on his shirt when he stumbled in the kitchen after pouring himself a mug. After he changed, one of his diamond cufflinks broke, setting off an expletive-laced tirade. A hole in the wall and an injured foot later, he collected himself and drove to work. However, he didn't reach his office before Preston flagged him down.

"If it's not good news, I don't want to hear it," Blunt growled.

"Spill your coffee on your shirt again, sir?"

Blunt eyed him closely. "Wipe that smirk off your face before I do it for you."

Preston's expression turned serious. "It's not good news, but you need to hear it."

"Not now," he said as he turned and continued walking down the hall.

"Sir, it's about Madeline Meissner. She's back, and this time she's making some new accusations that are sure to draw unwanted attention."

Blunt stopped, his back still to Preston. "I thought I told you to take care of her."

"I did. She's no longer employed by *The Post* and has been added to a blackball list by all the area media outlets."

"Yet, she's managed to find a way to still make trouble for me?" Blunt said as he turned to face Preston.

"Perhaps I underestimated her a bit, but she's taken to the Internet and has a blog set up called *Washington Whispers* that's growing exponentially in popularity. Some of the morning radio talk shows are starting to cite her blog posts."

"What did she say?"

"She wrote a post this morning that all but accuses you of killing Nancy Goetter and claims to have an admission from you."

Blunt's pulse quickened, and he closed his eyes. "I turned off her recorder during that interview."

"Maybe she had a backup."

Blunt glared at her. "*Sonofabitch!*"

"What did you say, sir?"

"I told her to go ask Nancy Goetter—or something like that?"

"Definitely not admissible in a court of law."

"She has no intention of getting this to a legal court—she wants me tried in the court of public opinion."

"That's far more damaging to what you're doing here."

"Exactly." Blunt paused for a moment. "And you're sure it's her who's running that site?"

"She's been careful not to put her name anywhere, but I had one of the aides analyze the writing and compare it to her *Post* articles. Based on the writing style and her apparent sources, I'm confident it's her."

Blunt stroked his chin. "Perhaps she needs additional incentive."

"I can make that happen, sir."

"Make it happen fast. We need to nip this in the bud before it creates more problems than I've got time for."

CHAPTER 32

HAWK WALKED INTO HIS CLASSROOM and scanned the familiar environment. Cracked paint on the walls, dusty floors, desks that looked like they'd been around since the 1950s, and a shoddily cleaned chalkboard. He'd never been in *that* particular room, but it looked like ones he'd been in before. The surroundings sparked both hope and despair in him. Hope that maybe he could help change those people's lives in some small way; despair that nothing would ever transform the country and her people who were little more than unshackled prisoners to the terrorists who governed with guns and bombs and fear. Would the Afghan people ever rise up and take their country back? Or did they even want to? Did they have any idea what kind of freedom the world held beyond the tightly-guarded sandbox?

There'd been no Arab spring in Zaranj—or any other part of Afghanistan. If those people were ever going to get a taste of freedom, someone was going to have to spoon feed it to them.

Just before 8 a.m., students began filing into the classroom, most of them with their heads down, staring at their smart phones.

I guess a few things have changed since I was last here. Looks just like home.

Hawk worried that with the proliferation of smart phones his cover could be in jeopardy. It's why he chose to operate in a disguise. For his whole life, Hawk battled fast sprouting facial hair, sporting a five o'clock shadow by noon. It was such a mind-boggling phenomenon that he wondered if someone sprinkled fertilizer on his face while he slept each night. But for once, it served him well. He used a costume beard for a few days until his own beard grew out enough that he could go *au natural*. If things this time went like they did last time, his beard would eventually get pulled by one of his students.

His introduction to English class contained fourteen students, most of which were under the age of twenty, all male. The youngest was a smart aleck kid named Kahlil who Hawk pegged to be about fourteen years old. Realizing he was the youngest, Kahlil wasted no time in using self-deprecating humor as a way to not only draw attention to himself but keep imminent mockery at bay.

However, it was a seventeen-year-old kid named

Raja Tawhid who grabbed Hawk's attention.

Raja handled himself differently than most of his classmates. Instead of viewing English as a fun subject and a way to get some of his questions answered about the country, he took it seriously. He scowled at classmates who made jokes. He stayed after class to talk further with Hawk about certain nuances of the language. At the end of the third week of classes, Hawk invited Raja to tea, and he accepted.

Hawk wasn't sure Raja would show up for their meeting after he was more than fifteen minutes late, but he finally did. Hawk didn't mind as he enjoyed watching the sun slip away on the horizon.

"I apologize, Mr. Wells," Raja stammered. "Is that the correct word?"

Hawk smiled and gestured for him to sit down. "It is, and if I were to give you a grade right now, it'd be an A-plus."

"That is good, no?"

Hawk leaned forward in his seat and laughed, slapping the table playfully. "Yes, that is the best possible score. Do you understand?"

Raja nodded and smiled. "I know what *best* means."

Hawk sipped his tea and set it down before locking eyes with Raja. "So, why do you want to learn English so badly? You're not like the other students."

"I want to understand Americans more."

"So you're curious about America?"

Raja looked down. "No. Not really. I think I know what it's like already."

"And what do you think it's like?"

"Guns. Alcohol. Sex. Greedy people. How do you say, *arrogant*?"

"You've just described a Hollywood movie, but that's not what it's really like."

Raja shifted in his seat. "So, tell me what a normal day is like for an American."

Hawk leaned forward in his seat and took a deep breath. "Many Americans have families, just like you do here in Afghanistan. They care about their children. They want to see them get educated. They want to live in peace and have the freedom to pursue their dreams. It's not all that different from what you want here. Most days, Americans go to work and come home and spend time with their families and friends."

Raja's eyes widened. "Are you sure?"

Hawk chuckled. "Yes, that's what most people do—what most people want. But it's not always so easy."

"No?"

"No, it's not. There are people who don't have an easy life. They don't have enough money to pay their bills or feed their families like they wish they could. They must do everything just to survive. It's difficult for them."

"That is what my family is like."

Hawk rubbed his beard. "Tell me about your family."

"My mother must work two jobs just to provide food for us after my father helped some U.S. soldiers but was shot two days later."

Hawk's eyes and forehead expressed sympathy. "I'm sorry to hear that. I didn't know."

"A neighbor shot him. He told my father that only a coward would help the Americans, and I agree with him."

Hawk shrugged. "I don't think everything is so easy to understand. Perhaps your father thought he was doing the right thing, as did your neighbor. Situations like these are never easy."

"Everyone I know has treated me like I have— what do you call it—a disease?"

Hawk nodded in agreement.

"So, I have a disease. I had a father who cared more for the Americans than he cared for his only family."

"Maybe he cared for the Americans *because* he cared for his own family."

"What do you mean?"

"Maybe he saw that helping the Americans was a way to help you in the future. Maybe he thought if the Americans won, then his family would have a chance to pursue their dreams."

Raja furrowed his brow and took a sip of his tea. Hawk could tell that the young man had never truly pondered why his father would've helped the Americans. At least, not positive reasons.

"Your father cared about you," Hawk said. "He wanted the best for you."

"You know nothing about my father."

"I know that he likely wanted you to experience a life full of opportunities he never had." Hawk paused for a moment. "Do you have any sisters?"

Raja nodded.

"Maybe he wants the best for them, too."

"Women are only good for cooking and cleaning and bearing children."

Hawk held up his hand and waved it dismissively at Raja. "I can tell you that's not true. Women can do so much more than that."

"Are you married?" Raja asked.

Hawk held up his left hand. "See," he said, pointing to his ring finger. "No ring. I'm not married. If you want to learn more about American culture, that's something you can keep in mind. Most married people wear a ring on *this* finger."

Raja shrugged. "A ring does not always tell the whole story."

"Neither does a first encounter with someone—and sometimes a second or a third. And when it comes to our enemies, making them less human and more evil is how we convince ourselves that our actions are justified."

"Do you see us as your enemy?"

Hawk shouldn't have been surprised by Raja's candor, but it still caught Hawk off guard coming from such a young man.

"Well, of course, not. I try to view everyone as my friend." He paused and took a deep breath. "But sometimes, there are people who pose great threats to others and those close to them. Those enemies are people I'd rather not get to know."

Raja smiled and raised his cup of tea. "Me, too. How do you say, 'I'll drink to that'?"

Hawk laughed. "Usually people say that with a glass of wine or beer, but since we're in Afghanistan, I guess a cup of tea can work, too." He set his cup down on the table in front of him. "So, who are these enemies you'd rather not get to know?"

"Maybe one day I'll tell you."

Hawk forced a smile and picked up his cup again. He suddenly had an uneasy feeling about his student.

***

THE NEXT DAY AFTER CLASS, Hawk decided to embark on a reconnaissance mission. With an hour before the noontime Dhuhr prayer, and not much in the way of intel, he decided to use his time wisely to gather as much information about Zaranj as possible and begin to covertly figure out where Nasim Ghazi's base of operations might be. And based off Raja Tawhid's chilling comments the day before, Hawk decided to follow him and see where he went.

Meandering somewhat aimlessly behind Raja, Hawk kept his eye on the kid at all times. At first, his stroll through the streets of Zaranj seemed harmless enough. He purchased a few items in the market, but it all seemed benign. A few strands of cloth, some string, a couple of loaves of fresh bread. Raja scanned the market and proceeded to slip into a small watch and clock repair shop. Then he vanished.

Hawk wondered how he could've lost Raja so quickly. There was no way he could've been made by a kid with no experience. From Hawk's perspective, Raja appeared to feel comfortable in his hometown, cruising around the market like he owned it, waving and saying hello to undoubtedly familiar faces. But something happened—Raja was gone.

CHAPTER 33

BY NATURE, GUY HIRSCHBECK tended to be careful about everything he did. He never turned on his car without first being buckled in properly. If there was a hint of rain in the forecast, he carried his compact umbrella with him that day. When flu season was in full swing, he kept a small stash of antibiotic wipes in his pocket for handling door knobs and faucet handles. So, it was curious that when he entered the world of espionage, he didn't incorporate more safeguards to protect him.

Perhaps taking the same route home every evening proved to be the safest way in Hirschbeck's mind. It also proved to be his undoing.

With a summer thunderstorm rolling across the Chesapeake Bay, Hirschbeck employed his windshield wipers, which swept furiously back and forth to maintain a clear field of vision. He pulled up to a stoplight and watched as the rain pelted the pavement, almost bouncing across the road. His phone rang, and he pushed the hands-free option on his steering wheel.

"This is Hirschbeck."

"Sir, I wanted to inform you that Senator Blunt has positioned one of his assassins in Afghanistan," said the man tasked with running his secret program.

"For what purpose?"

"It's unclear at this point, but we believe he's going after another Al Hasib asset."

Hirschbeck slammed his fist on the steering wheel. "That old man is going to set us back fifty years in foreign relations once this blows up in his face."

"Do we have any assets on the ground there?"

"There's a U.S. military installation in Zaranj, which was the assassin's last known location."

The light turned green, and Hirschbeck eased onto the gas. "No, that's too messy and difficult to explain. I'm thinking someone more covert."

"We do have an asset in Zaranj—a guy by the name of Frank Culbert. He's mostly just there to monitor local activity, more like an analyst than anything. Works with the Peace Corps as his cover."

"Think he can handle the job?"

"It might be a bit of a stretch."

"Task him with it and give me a full report. I want this taken care of within two weeks at the most. Tell him it's got to be neat and to let us know if he needs help with clean up."

"Roger that, sir."

Hirschbeck hung up and eased onto the brake pedal again as the traffic light tottering from a wire draped across the street turned red.

His phone rang again. He growled and answered it. "What?"

"Why so angry?" the other caller asked. "You ever consider taking yoga classes or looking into meditation?"

"I have considered quitting."

"Your country needs you, Senator. Besides, we put you here for a reason, and you must not forget why."

"Don't worry. I haven't."

"Excellent. So, how are things going with eliminating Senator Blunt's Project Z? Have you defunded him yet?"

"We hit a small snag there, sir."

"Oh?"

"Yes, the committee took fifty million from my project and gave it to his."

"Good thing you aren't really funded by that petty cash fund then, isn't it?"

Hirschbeck chuckled. "If he only knew."

"Well, inside jokes aside, this is still a setback."

"Yes, but we have a bead on Blunt's top operative, who we have reason to believe will be making a move soon."

"Good. Let's eliminate him as soon as possible. If we can't cut off the head of the snake, let's cut off its body."

"I'll keep you posted, sir."

Hirschbeck hung up and headed down the road again, exiting the city and climbing into the Virginia hills, where he lived on a secluded lot in a heavily wooded area. He navigated his car up the winding roads as the rain subsided.

When the car behind edged closer than he was comfortable with, he adjusted his rearview mirror, annoyed that the vehicle's bright headlights were making it difficult for him to see. He tapped his brakes a couple of time, hoping that the driver got the hint to back off. Instead, the car roared up behind him and tapped him.

Hirschbeck stomped on the gas and roared forward. And so did the car tailing him. It hit Hirschbeck twice more before driving him off the road and into a ditch.

When Hirschbeck's car came to a stop, it did so with a sudden thud against a Virginia oak. He fought off the airbag that had inflated from the steering wheel and tried to open the door. He couldn't since it was jammed due to the force of the hit that apparently bent the car's frame.

Hirschbeck slid into the passenger's seat and tried

to get out there. That door wouldn't budge either. However, the automatic window still worked. He depressed the button and the glass slid down. Hirschbeck pulled himself up and through the window. The rain returned, ripping through the canopy above with fierce determination.

The moment Hirschbeck's feet hit the forest floor a hard object hit him in the head. Knocked off balance, Hirschbeck tried to spin around and face his attacker, but he couldn't, instead tumbling to the ground.

The man pounced on top of Hirschbeck and rolled him over, pulling out a gun and jamming it into his forehead.

"Why are you doing this?" Hirschbeck asked. "I didn't mean to tap my brakes."

The man glared down at him. "This isn't about road rage."

"Then what is this about? Maybe we can work something out."

The man smiled and shook his head. "Senator Blunt sends his greetings."

Then he pulled the trigger.

CHAPTER 34

WHEN HAWK WENT DEEP COVER, Alex had more free time on her hands than she preferred. Instead of coordinating missions, she hacked databases and looked at ways to expose underground terrorist cells. It was a valuable way to spend her time, just not that exciting. The cyberspace world never held much allure for her despite how vital it was to the success of their missions.

She'd last heard from Hawk three weeks prior, and she wasn't sure when she'd hear from him again. Though she vowed to maintain a professional relationship, she struggled to keep herself from developing feelings for him. He was a globe-trotting assassin, and she knew there'd never be much of a life with him even if she ever had a chance. But that didn't stop her from letting her mind wander.

After she finished rooting out low-level terrorists online one afternoon, she decided to do some unauthorized snooping on Hawk. If she couldn't get to know him better in person, maybe she could find something to help her connect with him through personnel files.

As Alex started to look into a number of files with Hawk's name attached to them, she noticed something strange.

What is that all about?

Several of the files were restricted. Using her hacker prowess, she managed to crack a few of them. However, even within each file, there were still portions that remained classified as *top secret*, and figuring out a workaround proved to be a challenge.

Undaunted, Alex figured out a way past the firewalls preventing her from getting a look at the classified information.

At first, most of the information seemed benign. Then something caught her eye and made her gasp.

Hawk's never gonna believe this.

CHAPTER 35

WHEN RAJA TAWHID FAILED to show up for class after three days, Hawk decided to go to his house and find out what happened. A woman wearing a burqa answered the door.

"May I help you?" she asked in Pashto.

"My name is Simon Wells, and I'm Raja's English teacher," Hawk began in his best Pashto. "He hasn't been in class for three days, and I was concerned about him. Is he around?"

The woman turned her head and yelled, "Raja! Your teacher is here to see you."

She turned to face Hawk.

"Are you his mother?" Hawk asked.

She nodded.

"Your son is a good student."

"He works very hard."

Hawk heard a few soft giggles and looked behind her to see two young teenaged girls scampering down the hall. They weren't wearing burqas and were promptly scolded by their mother for allowing another man to see them without proper covering.

After a few moments of awkward silence, Raja slipped up behind his mother.

"What is it mother?" he asked.

"Your teacher is here to see you. He's been worried about you. Said you haven't been in class for three days."

Raja scowled. "He must be mistaken."

She turned toward her son and gestured toward Hawk. "Perhaps you can speak with him yourself about this mistake." She then shuffled away.

Raja slipped outside and joined Hawk on the stoop, shutting the front door.

"What are you doing here?" Raja asked in English. "An American coming to my house doesn't look good for me with the rest of my family."

"I was concerned about you. You haven't been to class in three days."

"I'm not getting a grade in the class, am I?"

Hawk shrugged. "It depends. Do you want one?"

"I appreciate you wanting to help and checking up on me, but I don't need you coming around here. It's not good for me or our family."

Hawk glanced around and noticed no one nearby paying particularly close attention to their conversation. Nevertheless, he decided to step out of plain sight. He tugged on Raja's shirt, gesturing for him to follow him around the corner.

"What do you want?" Raja asked once they were more hidden.

"I saw you vanish in the market a few days ago after class, and I don't think that you intended for that to happen, did you?"

Raja shook his head.

"Who were those men? And what did they want? I can help you if you're in trouble."

"You? Help me?" Raja looked away and stared in the distance. "You're just an English teacher. You don't know what these guys are like."

"What guys?"

"I shouldn't really talk about this."

Hawk put his hand on Raja's shoulder. "I'm your friend—your teacher. You can talk to me."

Raja drew back and crossed his arms; he seemed to contemplate whether or not he should say anything. He took a deep breath before he spoke. "I don't know if you can help, but I will tell you about what happened."

Hawk edged closer and bent down as Raja spoke in a hushed voice.

"My cousin drives a truck for an export company down to Chabahar in Iran twice a week. He lives in Delaram to the northwest of us, but I am his contact here. When people need special things imported, they make me call him and arrange for him to pick up goods for them."

"What if you were to refuse?"

"They would kill my mother and my sisters." He paused for a moment. "But I sometimes *want* to help them. And on this particular trip, I had to go with him."

"Did you want to help them the other day?"

Raja looked at his feet and kicked at the sand. "Maybe."

"What did they make you do?"

"It's not what they made me do—it's what they are doing."

"And what is that?"

"I can't talk about it. They'd hurt my family. But it's not good. Part of me wants to go along with them, but part of me doesn't. How do you say it? I'm *torn*?"

Hawk smiled and nodded. "Yes, *torn* is the right word if you are having a difficult time deciding between two things."

"It's very difficult for me."

"Are you sure you don't want to tell me? Sometimes it makes us feel better to share with a friend when we're struggling with a decision."

"I'm sorry, Mr. Wells, but I can't. Not now anyway."

"I understand," Hawk said. He patted Raja on

the back and walked away. But not too far. He needed to keep an eye on him.

***

AN HOUR LATER, Hawk watched from a nearby rooftop as Raja walked toward a small building about half a kilometer from his house. Raja strained as he pulled a cart covered with a blanket. During his conversation with Raja, Hawk had slipped a small bug with a tracker beneath the boy's collar.

Let's find out what this is all about.

At this point, Hawk's reconnaissance mission was hanging on by a thread. Not much in the way of intel had been learned nor had he been able to discover Nasim Ghazi's whereabouts. But he had a feeling that maybe Raja and the poorly-explained reason for his absence might lead him to Ghazi at best, at worst to some secret terror cell. Either way, there was nothing but upside for Hawk if he managed to gain some information out of this meeting.

Thinking quick on his feet, Hawk created a makeshift blind out of some clothes hanging on a line and a cardboard box lying nearby. It wasn't his best work on the fly, but it was sufficient in that moment.

He peered through his binoculars at the structure and jammed an earbud into his right ear to listen in.

Hawk watched Raja drop his cart and enter the building, the door creaking as it opened and shut. It sounded like Raja slid a deadbolt into place.

"Raja, did you bring what I asked?" came a familiar voice.

"Yeah, it's all there."

The sound of a deadbolt sliding was followed by the door opening. A man wearing a keffiyeh with his head down, popped outside, stooped over, and looked around. When he seemed convinced no one was there, he ripped the cloth off the top and smiled. Stacked high in the cart were blocks of C-4 explosives. The man re-covered the cart and pulled it inside. The door shut behind him again as the lock slid into place.

Hawk smiled to himself as he placed the voice. There was little doubt in his mind that it was Nasim Ghazi.

"In two days, I need your cousin to be here for a special delivery—one that is going to Kish."

"Kish?" Raja said. "His route doesn't go that way."

"We need a special favor."

"He can't do that. The truck belongs to the company he works for. He can't just drive it wherever he wants, especially to Kish."

"Tell him to get creative. Be persuasive. There will be a healthy compensation if he does. If not, there will be consequences."

There was a pause.

"I'm sure your cousin would rather take time off for this special trip than he would for a funeral."

"Okay, okay. I'll tell him."

Hawk watched the door swing open and Raja exit the building. Hawk gathered his belongings and stole across the roof and onto the ground, heading straight to a pay phone. He needed to call Alex.

CHAPTER 36

ALEX TIPPED BACK HER MUG to drain the final drop of coffee before leaving The Golden Egg and heading back to work. As she started to stand up, she felt a hand press down hard on her shoulder, forcing her back into her counter seat.

"Going somewhere?" came an ominous voice.

Alex turned around, relieved to see her friend Mallory from the CIA. Alex then shot Mallory a look. "Don't do that to me again, okay? I've had enough threats over the past few days."

Mallory shrugged but leaned in close to Alex. "Probably not the best way to say hello, but what other appropriate ways should fellow spooks say hello to one another?"

Another look.

Mallory slid into the seat across from Alex. "Never mind. Don't answer that."

Alex took a deep breath. "So, this is a nice surprise. What brings you here today?"

"I think you know that I always thought it was wrong what the agency did to you, but there wasn't anything I could do about it." Mallory slid a white letter envelope across the table to Alex. "Until now."

"What is this?" Alex said, cracking open the envelope and peering at the flash drive inside.

"Let's just say it's your get out of jail free card."

"So, this has nothing to do with what I've been working on?"

Mallory shook her head. "Not at all—well, at least, not that I know of." She paused and looked around the diner before continuing. "Let's just say if you ever run into any trouble with Simon Coker, this will make it go away—and go away quickly."

Alex held up the envelope. "Thanks for this. You have no idea what this means to me."

"It'll mean a whole lot more if you ever need it. Just remember that you didn't get it from me."

***

BACK IN HER OFFICE, Alex settled into the chair at her desk when her phone rang. She glanced at the "unknown" glaring back at her on the phone's small display screen. Who was on the other end determined how her day might go, and she was desperate for an easy day as she wanted to continue her research. She contemplated ignoring the call, but if it was Hawk, she needed to talk to him.

"This is Alex," she said after she finally picked up.

"Alex, this is Hawk. We need to talk."

"Yeah, we do. Big stuff happening that you need to be aware of."

"You're telling me. Something is going down in a couple of days. I don't know what, but it's big."

Alex leaned back in her chair and tapped her pen on her knee. "I think I know what it might be."

"What have you heard?"

"There's been some chatter about a possible attack in Bahrain."

"That makes sense based on what I'm about to tell you—but Bahrain? What would make a good target for terrorists there?"

"The U.S. Naval Forces Central Command, not to mention the Fifth Fleet."

Hawk gasped.

"What is it?" Alex asked.

"Al Hasib is going for their own version of Pearl Harbor."

"What makes you so sure?"

"I finally found Nasim Ghazi, and I saw what he's working on. Several hundred pounds of explosives are heading toward Kish along the Iranian coast in two days. If it makes it there, that C-4 is going on a boat to Bahrain—guaranteed."

"Think you can stop him?"

"I'm not sure when they'll be shipping it out, which pretty much means I have until tomorrow night to stop him."

"I'll notify Blunt."

"Are you sure that's a good idea? I don't want him calling in drones to destroy a truck as it treks across Iran, and I certainly don't think it'd be a good idea to bomb anywhere in Afghanistan with a drone."

"You don't trust him?"

"Do *you* after what he did last time?"

"Good point. I'll hold off on telling him until after you eliminate Ghazi and the threat. If I don't hear back from you by tomorrow evening, I'll have to tell him."

"Fair enough. I'll call you soon."

Hawk hung up and Alex exhaled. She didn't like keeping secrets from Blunt, but Hawk was right. The last time she clued him in, Blunt did exactly what the program wasn't supposed to do—unless she'd been manipulated into joining Firestorm under false pretenses.

Maybe that's just Blunt's way of getting me to go along with his plan. Maybe it's all a lie.

At that point, it didn't matter. If Hawk didn't stop Al Hasib's next attack, innocent American soldiers were going to lose their lives.

CHAPTER 37

HAWK RETREATED TO HIS HOME and began scheming. Since he knew where Nasim Ghazi was, killing him was the least difficult portion of Hawk's assignment. It was securing the explosive devices that presented him with the biggest challenge.

To do so, he needed help. And he wondered if it was a task Raja would willingly assist in. Hawk bristled at the idea of employing the same threatening tactics against Raja and his family that Ghazi and Al Hasib used. But if it was the difference in saving thousands of lives, Hawk decided he could live with it. He'd ask before he'd strong-arm Raja.

Then there was the issue of timing. If Raja's cousin arrived in two days time, that gave Hawk a small window to take action—and succeed. If Raja's cousin came too close to the time of the transport's arrival, he jeopardized the mission. If just one thing went wrong and he got captured, he knew those explosives would roll on down to Kish and wind up on a boat for Bahrain. The opportunity to thwart the attack would be gone, and Alex would be flying blind in D.C.

That left him with only one real viable opportunity—the next evening. If successful, he'd have enough time to dispose of the explosives and escape Zaranj before anyone else was the wiser. And the cover of night gave him the best chance at success. It also gave him the best chance to survive.

The Maghrib call to prayer started to echo throughout the city over the various mosques' loudspeakers. Hawk poured himself a glass of wine and sketched out rudimentary schematics of the building he'd observed Nasim Ghazi working in. With one more casual pass by the building in the morning on the way to class, Hawk would make his final determination regarding his approach.

***

THE NEXT MORNING, Hawk arose early and headed to class. With everyone observing morning prayer, the streets were relatively empty. Hawk thought to himself that if he were ever going to be a thief in a Muslim country, it'd be too easy to know when to strike. There'd be five good opportunities each day.

But Hawk wasn't planning on entering a life of

crime—he was simply intent on stopping it. And if he blurred the lines as he went, so be it. Courage when facing men with nothing to lose required a loose adherence to the rules of engagement. In Hawk's line of work, success was measured through results, not the means by which he took to get them. No family holding the bloodied and lifeless body of a loved one would care if he followed a litany of prescribed rules. An assassin's life was ruled by one thing and one thing only—eliminating the target.

Hawk shuffled past the building and circled it twice, making certain no one was watching him. He crept around the back and tried to peek in the dingy windows. Nothing. He only found one other entrance, a pair of large double doors. He surveyed it for a moment and made a mental note about how he would go about entering the facility and creating an inescapable kill box for Ghazi.

As he circled the building for a final time, he thought he heard a noise. A shadowy figured vanished behind a nearby house.

Someone was watching him.

CHAPTER 38

NASIM GHAZI RETURNED FROM PRAYERS with a fresh sense of mission. He'd been cooped up far too long for the past few weeks preparing for his most ambitious assignment yet. He'd spoken with Karif Fazil once through an encrypted website and once on the phone. The moment the explosives were on their way to Kish, he'd call him again to make sure Al Hasib's operatives could carry out the rest of the plan.

If it were up to him, he'd be there on site to witness firsthand the dramatic take down of a U.S. Naval ship. But he'd have to bask in the glory elsewhere and watch the news reports on television. If Al Hasib was successful, the number of people looking for Ghazi would increase exponentially. Perhaps a bounty would be placed on his head. And at this point, Fazil regarded him as the organization's most important asset.

But Ghazi knew better. He was the brains behind the operation, the reason for Al Hasib's modest success to this point. The general population around the world had likely never heard of Al Hasib nor knew who they were or what they stood for. But they would after this. There'd be articles written about them while television personalities opined about Al Hasib's motivation and reason for their success. And Ghazi would laugh at it all, knowing that the very people who would grow to hate him the most were the ones who not only made him that way, but also trained him.

A smile spread across his face at the mere thought as he soldered more wires in constructing another pound of C-4.

He thought about his long journey to get to that point—about all the people who disparaged Islam to his face, about how he buried Carl Butler a long time before. That period of his life seemed surreal, except for the pain. He'd strike back at the very heart of the thing those people who mocked him revered the most and believed to be invincible: the U.S. military. It'd be glorious as Ghazi imagined the imagery playing on televisions screens around the world behind somber newscasters. Meanwhile, he'd be dancing in the streets along with millions of his Muslim brothers.

His pleasant thoughts ended abruptly when someone rapped on the back door. Ghazi put down his equipment and crept toward the door with nothing but a knife in his hand. He peered through the crack before opening it.

"Raja!" he said. "What are you doing here?"

"It's about my cousin. He said he can't get access to a truck at work."

"Tell him I will take care of that for him," Ghazi said. "Just tell him to be on time and have his export license. I will make sure he has something to drive, and if he doesn't show up, tell him he better be getting as far away from here as possible. Because if I find him, I'll gut him."

Raja drew back as Ghazi pointed the knife at Raja. He nodded and exited quickly.

Ghazi pondered for a moment about alerting Fazil and aborting, but he eventually decided against it.

If he had to drive to Kish himself, he would. Nothing was going to stop him from putting Al Hasib on the international map.

Nothing.

CHAPTER 39

HAWK CALLED ROLL before he began teaching. Despite being labeled an introductory class, the majority of his students entered with a firm grasp of the English language. Over the prior few weeks, it had grown to an impressive understanding. And while he hoped they would utilize their new English skills in ways that would improve their lives, he discovered that they were instead using their knowledge to watch American reality television.

"The Kardashians? Why do you watch that crap?" Hawk asked.

One of the students raised his hand. "What does 'crap' mean? Is that like 'shit'?"

The classroom filled with nervous giggles and cackles.

Hawk sighed and shook his head. "I am here trying to teach you the essence of the English language, but you are only interested in the curse words."

"If we didn't know the curse words, we couldn't

understand what the Kardashians were trying to say," one girl blurted out.

"Why do American television shows have—how do you say it—*beeps* in the middle of someone talking?" another student asked. I find it extremely annoying."

Hawk smiled. "That's for the really bad curse words, the kind you wouldn't want your mother to hear you say."

The teenaged boy nodded and smiled. "I understand."

Hawk held up his hands. "Now, while I'd love to continue this fascinating discussion about the Kardashians and taboo words in English, we do have a lesson we need to begin. Are you ready?"

The class seemed more enthusiastic than usual with one notable exception: Raja Tawhid was nowhere to be found.

CHAPTER 40

RAJA SQUINTED TO KEEP the dust out of his eyes as he held the throttle open on his motorcycle. Goggles would've been preferable in such conditions, but he sweated more than most, which fogged up his view in less than a minute after putting them on. And that day was warmer than most. The bike didn't perform as well on pavement, but it didn't matter much with all the sand that constantly swept across the paved highway between Zaranj and Delaram. Raja's cousin, Tarik, would have to endure a three-hour journey sitting behind Raja, but he doubted either would care. Just getting Tarik to do Ghazi's bidding was what mattered most given the new ultimatum handed down.

Once Raja arrived in Delaram, he zipped along a series of narrow alleyways until he reached Tarik's house.

Raja knocked on the door. As soon as it swung open, he looked at his cousin. "Are you ready?"

Tarik took a deep breath and put his hands up.

"I don't know if I can do this."

Raja stepped inside, pushing his way past Tarik. "You don't know if you can do this? You don't know if you can do this? Are you crazy? You have no choice."

Tarik held his index finger to his lips. He gestured for Raja to move into another room away from the rest of Tarik's family who were engaged in watching a television show. "I've been thinking—I don't wish to do this any more. I'm done helping Nasim."

"You can't just quit working for Nasim. Do you know what's going to happen when I tell him that you won't come with me? There will be a dozen members of Al Hasib over here by sundown, and they'll kill you and your family."

"No, they won't," Tarik said, pointing at the luggage stacked near the door.

"You're leaving?"

"As soon as you leave, we're getting out of here."

"What about your job? And the rest of your family?"

Tarik slumped onto a small couch and buried his head in his hands. He sighed before he looked back up at Raja. "What kind of life is this, wondering when I'll get caught running contraband across the border into Iran? I can't live the rest of my life in fear. That's not living."

Raja eyed Tarik's export license lying on the table.

The opportunity presented him with a dilemma. On one hand, it gave him an opportunity to fulfill Nasim's demands in case Tarik remained stubborn. On the other, Tarik was likely counting on the license to help him sneak his family out of the country and vanish for good. Taking it could save his own life, but at the expense of Tarik's.

"What do you think is going to happen to the rest of your family? What do you think they're going to do to *me*?" Raja pleaded

Tarik stood and walked up to Raja and embraced him. "I love you, Raja, and I know you believe in what Al Hasib is doing. But it's not the life for me."

Raja smoothly snatched the licensed without Tarik noticing and sneered at him in disgust as Raja turned toward the door. "What kind of Muslim are you? This is jihad, and we must do what we can."

Tarik grabbed Raja by his arm, his fingers uncomfortably digging in. "This is not jihad. This is murder."

"It's no different than what the American soldiers have done to us."

"Then be better than them. Don't lower yourself to their level."

Raja seethed for a moment before striding toward the door and exiting the room.

"Raja!" Tarik said as he followed him outside.

Raja climbed onto his bike and kicked down hard as the engine rumbled to life. He held the clutch in while he revved the engine. It whined for a few seconds. Then Raja turned and looked at Tarik.

"Good luck," Raja said. "Don't blame me when they come looking for you. It's your choice, but you can still change your mind."

Tarik reached over and hugged Raja. "I can't. And while you may not understand my decision now, you will years from now. It will make sense one day."

Raja sighed and released the clutch, tossing dirt in Tarik's direction and speeding away. He dreaded delivering the bad news—both for Tarik and himself.

CHAPTER 41

HAWK CLOSED ONE EYE and stared down the barrel of one of his guns. If there was one thing he'd learned about being an assassin, it was that preparation was the key to a clean get away. With everything working properly, a well-executed plan resulted in an easy day at work. And that included his guns firing without a hitch. He'd spent enough time in the Middle East to know that he couldn't clean his gun enough due to the ever-present dust and sand.

In thirty minutes, the sun would slip beneath the horizon, and it'd be time to do what he came there to do: kill Al Hasib's master bomb maker—and, if the reports were to be believed, Al Hasib's real mastermind. Hawk figured he might get lucky and help Raja escape a life of terrorism, one that'd be undoubtedly short.

Hawk finished cleaning his last gun when a knock startled him. "Coming," he said as he stashed all the guns in his bedroom.

He hustled toward the door and was about to unlock it when he noticed one of his handguns still lying on the kitchen counter. He shoved it in the front of his pants to avoid any printing that might draw suspicion.

However, he sighed in relief when he peeked through the window and saw who it was.

"Frank!" Hawk said as he opened the door and welcome the local Peace Corps coordinator. "It's been a while. Come on in."

Frank Culbert lumbered inside without saying a word.

Though Hawk hadn't been sure what to make of his supervisor after his first meeting, he didn't raise any red flags after a cursory vetting. Just a guy who once thought he'd better the world by working with the Peace Corps and discovered more meaning abroad than at home. However, his surprise visit was equally curious and coincidental to Hawk.

"So, what brings you here tonight?"

Culbert glanced around the apartment and leaned against the counter. "I just wanted to stop by and see how things were going. Usually, volunteers show up at the weekly support gatherings at my house, especially the new ones. But you haven't made one yet. I wanted to make sure you were handling everything okay and weren't homesick or depressed."

"I can assure you that everything is fine, and I appreciate you checking up on me, I really do."

Culbert paced around the kitchen for a moment, clasping his hands together, his head bowed as if in thoughtful meditation. "I have a feeling there's something else to your reason for being here."

"Really? Such as?"

"I think you're true intention for being in Zaranj has nothing to do with the Peace Corps."

Hawk forced a chuckle and threw his hands in the air in surrender. "Okay, Frank, you got me. My dad runs a weapons manufacturing company back in the states. But I can tell you that I'm not here looking for new buyers for him, if that's what you're worried about."

Culbert's eyes narrowed. "If I was worried about that, you'd already be dead."

Hawk's pulse quickened. Perhaps he'd misread Culbert. In an instant, he appeared far more menacing that he imagined. "Hey, now, that's not a very comforting thing to hear from your Peace Corps supervisor."

"I'm not here to comfort you."

Hawk eyed him closely. "Then what are you here for?"

Without answering, Culbert swung his leg around in a full roundhouse kick that nearly caught Hawk off guard. However, he leaned back and avoided any contact.

Culbert regained his balance after the missed kick and slid toward Hawk's knees, knocking him off balance. Hawk teetered for a moment before crashing to the floor. As he attempted to get up, Hawk stopped short when Culbert put his foot on Hawk's chest and whipped out a handgun.

"Is this how you treat all your volunteers?" Hawk asked. "Because this is a little strange, if you ask me."

Culbert forced an awkward grin. "To answer your question, I came here to kill you."

CHAPTER 42

RAJA TAWHID SKIDDED to a stop outside Ghazi's workshop. He climbed off his motorcycle and stared at the semi-truck parked outside. After a deep breath, he walked toward the door and knocked on it several times. A guard opened the door and ushered him in after Ghazi yelled his approval from the back of the building.

"Where's your cousin?" Ghazi asked as he marched toward Raja.

"He couldn't make it."

"Couldn't make it? Do you understand that's not an option?"

Raja nodded. "He got called into work at the last minute for a trip north."

Ghazi began raging around the room, yelling and screaming a string of expletives in both English and Pashto. He stormed toward Raja. "Do you know what this means? It means we're screwed. No more mission. No more revenge on those nasty Americans. No more justice." He paused as he continued to pace for a moment. "Call your cousin and ask him to reconsider."

"I would, but he left the moment I did."

"Call him again."

"There might be another way," Raja pleaded.

Ghazi cocked his handgun and pointed it at Raja. "I'm not interested in another way. Call him now, and put the call on speakerphone."

Raja could feel his throat tighten and his forehead begin to bead up with sweat. He prayed underneath his breath that Tarik wouldn't answer.

"I'm not going to reconsider," Tarik said after he answered.

"Say, 'Reconsider what?'" Ghazi whispered into Raja's ear.

"Reconsider what?" Raja asked.

"You know what I'm talking about. But if I need to tell you more plainly—I'm not going to help Nasim Ghazi any more."

Outraged, Ghazi ripped the phone out of Raja's hands and ended the call. "Clever. Covering for your lazy cousin—your spineless, gutless cousin who is afraid to do whatever it takes to advance the mission of Islam." He looked at one of the guards in the warehouse. "Call Fazil and ask him if he can get a team of men to pay Tarik a visit."

The man nodded and retreated to the back of

the room and began dialing on his cell phone.

"I have another idea," Raja said. "Please don't do that. Listen to me."

Ghazi waved him off. "There's no room for compromise when it comes to the cause—only commitment. What your cousin did was inexcusable."

"I stole his export license before I left his house," Raja said as he dug it out of his pocket and held it up.

"The border patrol agents will know it's not him. He travels there every week."

"I'll make up an excuse, tell them I'm filling in for him in a pinch because his daughter is sick and he needs to be with her but didn't want to lose his job."

Ghazi took a deep breath. "Interesting."

"It's our only option."

"It's our only option because you screwed up the mission," Ghazi said, the rage returning. "You were supposed to bring back Tarik. And you failed. You failed Al Hasib."

Raja raised his hands in surrender and knelt behind one of the nearby tables covered with C-4 explosives. "We don't have to abort the mission. We can still come up with a way to get the explosives across the border and into Chabahar. If you'll just trust me."

"Trust is something I'm running very short on these days."

CHAPTER 43

WHILE HAWK WAS ACCUSTOMED to being the hunter as opposed to the prey, he wasn't completely unprepared. Frank Culbert never once gave off the vibe that he was militarily trained. An NGO supervisor? Yes. But an operative for the government? Hawk never picked up on it.

But he had no time to waste wondering how he could've failed to properly vet the man now standing over him with a foot on his chest and a gun trained on him. It was time to turn the tables.

Instead of responding to Culbert's ominous statement, Hawk rolled left and drove his fist into the side of Culbert's knee. As Culbert started to buckle due to the pain, Hawk delivered a nasty blow to Culbert's crotch.

It didn't stop Culbert from firing his first shot at Hawk, which whizzed right past his head as he was knocked off balance. The second shot hit Hawk in the bicep—a sign that his attacker was aiming for center mass. It was shoot to kill all the way.

Hawk used the kitchen table as a momentary shield before he dove toward the living room and crouched behind the couch.

By that time, Culbert regained his balance and was muttering to himself. Then to Hawk, "The charade is over. I know you're a plant and not a real Peace Corps member."

Hawk kept his mouth shut and fished his gun out of the front of his pants. He wormed his way across the floor to the other side of the couch and took aim at Culbert, who still seemed stunned by the fact that he hadn't killed Hawk.

Two shots, center mass. It was all over.

Culbert hit the floor with a thud as blood spilled out around him. Gasping for air, he tried to say something as Hawk looked down at the man. But Hawk didn't have time to stoop down and listen to the dying man's last words. Instead, he pumped two more shots into his head, ending his suffering.

Hawk entered the bathroom and began to shave. The hair drifted downward, half of it landing in the sink while the other half landed softly on the floor. It was a symbolic gesture but also one that gave him time to think about how he was going to complete his mission. He was done with his charade as a teacher, and there was only one thing left to do.

On his way out of the house, he stepped over Culbert's body and was clear when he noticed something sticking out of his shirt pocket. He bent down and pulled it out. It was the same picture he'd lifted off the man who'd try to kill him on the rooftop in Kirkuk. He shoved the picture back into his pocket and exited the apartment.

The sun had just disappeared. There was no time to waste if he intended to stop Nasim Ghazi.

CHAPTER 44

HAWK NEVER STOPPED MOVING the moment he stepped outside into the evening streets of Zaranj. He'd equipped himself with enough weapons and artillery to withstand a prolonged gunfight with Ghazi and other Al Hasib operatives. He just hoped it would be enough.

Once he reached a perimeter of about a hundred meters outside Ghazi's workshop, Hawk slowed to a brisk walk and pulled his keffiyeh tight around his face. He didn't want to draw attention to himself and attract gunfire before he reached the front door of the facility.

He noted two armed guards milling around the main entrance. Using the barrel of their guns, they pointed at Raja's parked bike while they glanced around in a nonchalant manner. His Navy Seal training told him to isolate the men from one another to avoid creating a scene—and he found it to be a useful rule of thumb.

Hawk hurled a rock south of where the men were standing, gaining their attention. One guard went to check it out, leaving the other guard alone near the main entrance. Hawk slipped up behind the guard at the door and snapped his neck in one smooth motion.

Moments later, when the other guard returned from his fruitless investigation, he saw his partner crumpled on the ground. He rushed over to him and knelt down to check for a pulse. When he didn't immediately find one, he looked up in an obvious effort to identify where his attacker was positioned.

He never saw Hawk, who broke the man's neck within a second of grabbing him from behind.

Hawk dragged their bodies behind a nearby truck and crept near a window emitting light from Ghazi's workshop. Inside, he saw Ghazi raging about something while pointing his gun at Raja and also counted three other guards.

It wasn't great odds, but he'd take them, considering that instead of four-to-one odds, it was six-to-one odds a mere two minutes ago.

You got this.

With only two entrances to access the workshop, Hawk knew which one to choose—the one that would bring the most surprise. They wouldn't suspect for a minute that Hawk would walk in the front door, especially after there wasn't a single sound to alert them that danger lurked in the shadows.

He flung the doors open and opened fire immediately. Raja was to his left, and Hawk shoved the boy to the ground and pushed him with his foot in the direction of a table that would provide him with some cover during the gunfight.

Ghazi dove to the right, while his guards laid down cover for him.

"Mr. Wells? What are you doing here? You're screwing everything up," Raja said.

"Too late now, kid," Hawk said, pausing to fire back. "It looked like he was about to shoot you."

"I can take care of myself."

"It didn't look like you were doing such a great job to me."

Hawk popped up from behind the table and fired off several rounds, dropping one of the guards in the back. He glanced back at Raja. "You don't look too surprised to see me." He rolled to his right and put a bullet between the eyes of another guard and then another. Only Ghazi remained.

"I know who you are," Raja said. "Nasim showed me a photo of you before you arrived—one without your beard. He was going to kill my family unless I gave you up."

"And you agreed?"

Raja nodded.

Hawk held his index finger to his lips and crept to the side as the gunfire subsided. He caught a reflection of Ghazi on the glass.

"Don't be a coward. Come out in the open and die like a man," Hawk called out.

Ghazi remained frozen, but Hawk felt something else moving behind him. He turned just in time to throw his hand up to stop Raja from bashing him in the side of the head with a crowbar. He yanked it out of Raja's hand and put him in a sleeper hold, knocking him out.

"It's over!" Hawk called. "Your men are dead. The boy's out cold. And I know you're too much of a coward to strap on a suicide vest."

The challenge was too much for Ghazi to ignore as he stormed out of his hiding spot.

Hawk needed only one shot to fell him, dropping him before he took three steps in the open. Ghazi's body smacked the concrete floor hard, and his gun tumbled from his hand.

Hawk rushed over to him and knelt next to his body. He checked his pulse—Ghazi was gone.

He smiled to himself, satisfied that he'd accomplished his ultimate mission. He was lazier when it came to checking the bodies of the other three guards, instead choosing to fire close range shots at their heads. Walking toward the back of the shop, he opened a pair of sliding doors to reveal a sight that horrified him. Hundreds of pounds of C-4 explosives stacked five feet high. There was little doubt he'd saved hundreds of people's lives, whatever the target was.

Hawk heard movement near the front of the shop, and he rushed over toward it. Raja rubbed his head as he staggered to his feet.

"That's not a polite way to treat your teacher," Hawk said.

Raja stared at him with a blank expression on his face. "Ghazi was going to pay me fifty thousand dollars—my cousin's share—if I took all of this to Chabahar for him."

Hawk titled his head to one side and forced a smile. "You're made for more than this."

"You American pigs think you know better than everyone else," Raja said as he started to pace about. "You just storm into countries uninvited and take whatever you want."

"Raja, I watched you closely. You're a smart kid with a bright future ahead of you—as long as it's a future without these terrorists interfering with your life. They will tell you lies to accomplish their purposes, none of which will actually benefit you in the end. Your English is incredible, and you know so much already about the world. You'd be better off forgetting about these people."

"What do you know about me? I can't go any-where. I have no father. I must work to help support my mother. Until Ghazi offered me more money than I ever dreamed of making, I had no future. But you had to—how do you say—*screw it up*?"

"You'd be surprised how much I know about you, and how much I see of myself in you."

Raja smirked. "So I am to become a special forces warrior, an assassin for the American govern-ment? Is that my future?"

"That's not what I see in you. I see someone with potential, but you must learn to harness it for a good purpose."

"Like you? Killing people in a foreign country?"

Hawk grabbed Raja by the collar and dragged him toward the back of the workshop. "Tell me what you see."

"Explosives," Raja said.

Hawk let go of Raja's collar forcefully before pushing him back a couple of meters. "I killed a few men who were going to kill hundreds of innocent peo-ple, and they were going to kill them for a misguided cause. I saved hundreds more than I killed today, and these men were hardly innocent. That's why I do what I do. I use my skills to make sure more boys in both my country and other countries don't grow up without their fathers. It's pretty damn noble, if you ask me."

Raja stood there, unable to say anything, clearly overwhelmed by his emotions. Tears started to streak down his face before he choked out a few words. "I was going to kill you, but now—"

Hawk put his arm around Raja. "Nobody else needs to die today. Come on. Let's get you home. I'm sure your mother is worried about you."

CHAPTER 45

THE NEXT MORNING, Hawk awoke from his bed at the U.S. military compound on the outskirts of Zaranj. After he had returned Raja home, he called Alex, who arranged for an extraction by the U.S. military at the airbase nearby. Blunt had to call in two special favors to make it happen, but everyone was happy to oblige, considering the results.

"Are you ready to leave?" one of the guards asked Hawk after he finished his breakfast.

"I am." Hawk took a long sip of his coffee. "But I need to go back into Zaranj."

"Are you crazy? I can't take you back there."

"I made a promise to a guy who helped me catch one of the most wanted terrorists in the world, and I intend to fulfill that promise. If you have any questions about this, check with your commanding officer. It's already been cleared by the U.S. State Department."

"What exactly are we doing?"

Hawk smiled. "Lead me to your jeep. I'll tell you on the way."

***

AS THEY DROVE along the dusty road, Hawk shared with the soldier about the promise he'd made to the mysterious Mr. Angel. Once they arrived at their destination, Hawk hopped out of the vehicle.

"Don't worry. This won't take long. They'll be expecting us."

Hawk shuffled toward the house and knocked on the door.

"Yes?" said a woman as the door creaked open.

"Gulpari?"

"Yes? Who are you?"

"Eric Angel sent me to pick you up. I'm the one who contacted you last night." He glanced inside and saw her bags packed.

A young boy slipped up next to her and leaned against her leg. She rubbed his head and then gently lifted his chin so she could see his eyes. "Kamaal, it's time to get your things. We're leaving now."

Hawk grabbed the woman's bag and the little boy's hand, leading them to the waiting jeep. They climbed inside and left a trail of dust behind them. Hawk glanced over his seat at the boy, who remained stoic. His mother wiped away a streaking tear and tried not to cry.

"I never thought he would come and get us," the woman said. "I thought I would spend the rest of my life in shame here."

Hawk smiled at her. "Things are going to be very different for you now—very different. But I hope things will be better."

He glanced down again at the little boy. He couldn't help but notice just how much he looked like Eric Angel.

CHAPTER 46

BLUNT'S EYES DARTED back and forth as he read the story splashed across the front page of *The New York Times*. He couldn't resist a slight grin as he read his name. His grin grew bigger when he glanced at the article's author: Madeline Meissner.

Her story detailed how a special operation resulted in the elimination of one of the most notorious Muslim terrorists—and U.S. traitors—in the world. It also spoke of how it crippled Al Hasib and its ability to commit atrocities on a large scale basis. Another foreign policy expert was quoted as saying that the death of Nasim Ghazi would return Al Hasib to nothing more than a small regional player in the hierarchy of terrorism.

Blunt found another article just below the fold that was of special personal interest. "Senator Killed in Carjacking" blared the headline. The story told about how Senator Guy Hirschbeck was the victim of a random carjacking by a drug addict who'd just been released from prison. The report also mentioned the strange irony that the alleged carjacker had been one of the first criminals released early from prison based on a bill sponsored by Senator Hirschbeck himself.

"Ain't that a kick in the pants," Blunt said aloud.

"Excuse me, sir?" Preston said as he slipped into Blunt's office unnoticed.

"Sorry, Preston, I didn't see you there. Just commenting on this article."

"Good news, I trust."

"Good news for us—not so much for Senator Hirschbeck."

"Did something happen to him?"

"He's dead. Killed by one of those crack heads he insisted needed to be released early to stop overcrowding in prisons because they weren't violent offenders."

"Well, I'm sure he'd change his mind now given the chance."

Blunt folded the paper and slapped it down on his desk. He gestured for Preston to have a seat.

"Thanks for taking care of Madeline Meissner for me," he said. "She's a damn good journalist. And I enjoyed reading her article on the front page of *The New York Times* this morning."

Preston leaned back in his seat. "Well, it's like you always say, sir. Sometimes you just need to apply the right kind of pressure."

Blunt chuckled. "A quarter of a million and a job at the country's most prestigious daily newspaper trumped death threats, I suppose."

"For the time being," Preston said. "But I'm keeping my eye on her."

"Good," Blunt said. "A reporter in your pocket is always a good thing, and a tight leash is of utmost importance."

"I'm glad we're on the same page about this." Preston nodded and stood before heading toward the door. He stopped just short and looked over his shoulder. "You truly are an American treasure, sir."

Blunt waved him off. "Just doing my job to keep America safe."

Preston furrowed his brow. "So, just to be clear—you had nothing to do with Hirschbeck's unfortunate demise?"

"Not a thing, though I'm sure I'll muster up some tears for the funeral."

"Nice how that worked out for you then, sir."

Blunt leaned back in his chair and nodded. "I'm certainly not complaining."

CHAPTER 47

HAWK AGREED TO MEET Alex in the cafeteria of The National Archives building in College Park, Maryland. He hated D.C. traffic and the paranoia that he felt the moment he set foot in the city. But the National Archives was perfect for a public meeting place. It was heavily monitored, more remote and wide open. If anyone was surveilling them, he'd know it.

He settled into a corner booth a few minutes before 10 a.m. and awaited Alex's arrival. When Alex appeared from around the corner on the hour, Hawk was taken aback by her appearance. He'd seen her on video conferencing, but pixels on a screen didn't convey her power, grace, and beauty. Alex was dressed sharp with a white blouse and a long skirt, her head held high, confident. The fact that she was stunningly beautiful was just a bonus. He tried to look past the wavy brown hair that cropped her goddess-like face and her deep-set green eyes. She almost made him forget about Emily.

He stood when she arrived, gesturing for her to sit down.

"Thanks for meeting me," she said.

"My pleasure. I wouldn't turn down a face-to-face meeting with you after everything you've done for me."

"Even though Blunt told us never to meet in person?"

Hawk smiled and leaned forward, talking in almost a whisper. "We're *his* spies, remember?" He paused and glanced around the almost vacant room. "Besides, I scoped this place out before you arrived." He nodded in the direction of the only other two men in the room, both sitting together. "They're both employees who work in the microfilm research room. I doubt they've even bothered to notice that we are sharing the same air as them right now."

Alex laughed and flipped her hair over her shoulder.

"So, what is it you wanted to talk about?" Hawk asked. "It seemed quite urgent when you called."

"I'm glad you went dark when you did because I had some harrowing encounters with some other nefarious agents."

Hawk's eyes widened. "I had no idea. Are you okay?"

"I'm fine now, but it was touch and go for a while

there. Fortunately, I have a friend at the CIA who helped me get through it."

"Is that what you wanted to tell me about? Are you still in danger?"

"No, I took care of it—and some of the problems took care of themselves."

"So, what is it then?"

Alex took a deep breath. "While I was trying to figure out who was behind some of these attacks on me, I started digging in some places I probably shouldn't have and stumbled upon some information that I thought you'd want to know about."

"Out with it, Alex. I have enough drama in my life without you dragging this out."

She forced a smile. "Look, I don't really know how to say this other than your father isn't who you think he is."

"Is he some heartless criminal on top of being the world's foremost weapons manufacturer?"

"No, maybe I'm not putting this clearly, but Thomas Colton isn't your father at all."

Hawk withdrew, slumping back against the seat as he tried to process what Alex just said. After a few moments, he finally spoke. "Are you sure?"

"Unless the file was a plant for me to find, but I couldn't think of a legitimate reason for anyone to do that."

"So, who is my father?"

She shrugged. "I'm still working on that. There's no photo, and his file only has a number assigned with it—no name."

"But how can that be? My mother won a paternity suit against him. Surely, he didn't just concede that she was right without taking a paternity test. I mean, why else would he act like my dad?"

"Maybe your mom paid someone to alter the DNA test results. I don't know."

"So, the man you say is my real father is somehow connected to the CIA? That's where you found his file, right?"

She nodded. "It was a file I found attached to yours and under known relationships, you were listed as his son."

"That just seems like a mistake. I have a hard time believing that's true."

"I can do some more digging, but I thought you'd want to know. Perhaps you can ask Mr. Colton if he'd like to submit to another DNA test."

Hawk shook his head. "If I did that, my mother would lose everything she gets from him. And she deserves it for raising me on her own."

"Well, I won't tell you what to do with the information, but I thought you should know."

Hawk sighed. "I know this might be a lot to ask

on top of what you just told me, but can you find out the origin of these photos for me?" He slid her photos he'd collected off the would-be assassin in Kirkuk and Frank Culbert in Zaranj.

She picked them up and studied them for a moment. "I'll see what I can do." She glanced at her watch. "Look, I really need to run. I've got a debriefing with General Johnson and Blunt later today that I need to get ready for."

Hawk thanked her and watched her walk away. He was hoping the big secret she planned to tell him had something to do with stopping terrorism—or a sinister D.C. scandal. That he could've handled, possibly even enjoyed. But not this. Finding out that the man he believed to be his father wasn't created angst.

However, it also made him wonder. Who was his real father? And what was his story? And why did his mother lie all these years?

Those were questions he'd want answers to over time, along with the whereabouts of Emily's killers. He started to enter into a mental fog thinking about it all when the newscaster on the television in the corner said something that arrested his attention. His head snapped toward the direction of the screen.

More unrest in Sierra-Leone today as American Diamond magnate Theodore Barrister was shot and killed in Freetown this morning, resulting in the looting of his mine. This is

the second such incident at a diamond mine in West Africa this
month. In other news, oil continues to drop and reached a 35-
year low today.

Hawk grabbed his jacket and stood. He had some
more work to do.

THE END

Keep reading to get the first part of **DEEP
COVER**, Book 2 in the Brady Hawk series ...

DEEP COVER
Book 2

Yokodu, Sierra Leone

HAWK SWALLOWED HARD and tried to ignore the sharp blade held firmly against his neck. Only moments ago he was enjoying a drink with Jay, an expatriate who'd relocated to Sierra Leone for a job with a local safari outfit. It was a welcome conversation, especially after Hawk had been hidden in plain sight for almost a week. But the moment they exited the shanty riverside bar, something Hawk said apparently made Jay jumpy—and now Hawk had to consider the fact that each thought might be his last unless he calmed him down.

"Can we talk about this?" Hawk said.

"What's there to talk about, *Mister Martin*? As if that's even your real name," Jay snapped as he shoved

Hawk against the side of the building. "Want to tell me again about that duiker you killed?" He threw his head back and laughed. "Am I supposed to be scared?"

"I was just makin' small talk, man. Come on. No need to get all worked up about it."

"You think it's sporting to kill a defenseless little duiker in the wild—a little defenseless animal?"

"Seems like we have some cognitive dissonance going on here, Jay. I've got no weapon and you've got a knife to my throat."

"Shut up," Jay said as he tightened his grip on Hawk's arms. "I know why you're here and I'm going to collect quite a price for you."

"I wouldn't advise that, if I were you."

"I said, 'Shut up!'" Jay said, pushing Hawk forward into the dusky night air.

"Where are you taking me?"

Jay kneed Hawk viciously in the back of his leg, crippling Hawk for a moment and sending him to the ground. "Perhaps I should cut off your ears first since they seem to be a couple of appendages that don't work all that well."

Hawk felt the sandy soil grinding beneath his feet as they edged farther away from the bar, the darkness growing thicker with each step. A small outhouse a few meters ahead seemed large enough to provide any cover he might need, not to mention solving his dilemma of where to stash a body in a hurry.

Hawk staggered toward the outhouse and bumped it hard with his elbow. It was empty.

"Stay with me, Mister Martin," Jay said.

Hawk's captor jerked him back upright. However, the moment they cleared the outhouse, Hawk whirled and delivered a swift roundhouse kick to Jay's head. The man groaned as he fell forward, clutching his face. Two more powerful kicks to the rib—one crackled like a fire fueled by green wood— and Jay was done. Hawk then punched his assailant in the face, knocking him out.

In a way, Hawk felt sorry for him, saddened over the fact that this man's path had come to an end. *Wrong time, wrong place.* But it was an easy call—him or this expat who was about to kill him or worse: out him to a local terrorist. Hawk grabbed the man by the nape of his neck and then positioned himself behind Jay— and twisted until he heard a *crack*. Hawk picked up Jay's limp body and moved it into the outhouse. Once he situated Jay on the toilet, Hawk slit Jay's wrist so he began to bleed out. It'd look like a suicide—and no local law enforcement was going to think twice about looking into the death of an obnoxious American, even if the circumstances seemed odd.

He was almost through the door when he

stopped and turned back to look at him. The blood dripped hard and fast from his wrist and onto the dirt floor.

He wouldn't be the last person he'd kill on this mission. Hawk had a job to do and there was no margin for error.

CHAPTER 1

Two Weeks Earlier
Lake Anna, Virginia

BRADY YANKED ON HIS FISHING ROD and started to wrestle with what he initially believed to be a fish. But after a few moments, it was painfully obvious that he'd snagged his line on some debris. It'd been nearly fifty years since Virginia's power company flooded the area to cool the nearby nuclear power plant—and there was still plenty of garbage along the lakebed.

He whipped his rod back and forth for a few seconds in an effort to free the line before it snapped. Hawk snarled as he reeled in the rest of the twine and rummaged through his tackle box for another weight and lure. Behind him, a slow clap began. But he didn't have to turn his head. The cigar smoke gave away his visitor two minutes earlier.

"Blunt," Hawk said, his back still turned to the

senator. "What are you doing here?" He bit hard on his fishing line, severing it before threading the line through a new weight.

Maintaining his deliberate stride, Blunt continued toward him as his heavy footfalls on the dock echoed off the water.

Hawk stopped his repair work and looked over his shoulder, glaring at Blunt. "I think I asked you a question."

Blunt came to a stop about a meter away from Hawk. "Questions don't always deserve answers."

"Mine do. At least, if you want me to keep working for you, they do."

Blunt pulled the cigar out of his mouth and stared out across the lake. Fishing boats and jet skis dotted the glassy water, the hum of the motors barely audible from the dock. On the horizon, the sun was slipping away for the evening.

"These people have no freakin' idea how good they've got it," Blunt said before stuffing his cigar back in his mouth. "They're livin' a fairy tale thanks to people like me and you."

Hawk stood up and stared Blunt in the eyes. "What do you want?"

Blunt turned his back on Hawk and started to saunter down the dock. "Same thing as you, I suppose—world peace, a big bank account." He paused. "Power."

Hawk tightened his fishing line and returned his attention to Blunt. "We don't share the same ambitions."

"That's a shame, Hawk. That's a damn shame. I thought you were gonna be my guy for a long time."

"Excuse me for not returning your affinity," Hawk growled. "That's kind of how I am when people lie to me."

"Who's lying to you, Hawk?"

"Don't play games with me. You know good and well that you've hidden the truth from me."

"Hiding is not the same as lying."

"It is when you let me believe a lie—especially since it had to do with who my father really was. The fact that you allowed me to believe that Tom Colton, the U.S. military's most revered weapons maker, was my father makes you one twisted man. Every kid should know his father—at least know who he is."

Blunt slowly raised his eyebrows and nodded. "I figured you'd eventually find out one day."

Hawk huffed. "Helluva way to build trust—just let the sucker discover it on his own."

Blunt took the cigar out of his mouth and blew several rings. "However you may feel about what I did, just know that I was protecting you."

"Protecting me? From the truth?"

"If you ever get to be in a position like mine, you'll

quickly learn that achieving success on a mission is far more important than making sure everybody knows everything that's going on. I stopped caring about people's feelings a long time ago."

Hawk cinched his line and then cast it back into the water. "I'm not asking for a shoulder to cry on—just some straightforward talk."

"Fine. What do you want to know about your father?"

"Everything. Start at the beginning."

"I'm afraid most of it is classified."

"What can you tell me? Can you at least tell me his name?"

"Franklin Foster. Your father and I worked together in the CIA."

Hawk reeled in his line slowly. "Partners? You've gotta be kidding me?"

Blunt shook his head. "Nope. We worked together regularly, gathering intel on foreign diplomats and foiling assassination plots. Those were some good times."

"So, what happened to him?"

"*That* is what's classified."

"This is bullshit. It's not like I've got anyone to tell. I just wanna know."

"Look, Hawk, I know this isn't what you want to hear right now, but in due time I'll tell you everything. In the meantime, I need your help—Firestorm needs your help."

Hawk sighed. "You *will* tell me about my father."

"In time, I promise."

"Fine. Why don't you tell me why you're here. I knew this wasn't a social call from the moment I smelled your cheap Dominican cigar."

Blunt pulled the cigar out of his mouth and inspected it. "I need you to deal with a situation brewing in Sierra Leone. A diamond exporter by the name of Musa Demby. We've got intel that he's working with Al Hasib, bank rolling their operation with black market diamonds now that oil has gone in the tank."

"What's the mission?"

"Find out if this is indeed what Mr. Demby is up to. Secure the diamonds. Lay waste to his operation— you know, the usual. I've already got Alex working on a legend for you."

"So, no school teacher this time?"

"Oh, no. You should have more fun this time around. You're going to be a New Zealand exporter on a big game hunt."

"When do I leave?" Hawk asked.

Blunt took a deep breath and turned westward. The sun gleamed as it flashed its final beam of the day and sank for good.

"In a couple days," Blunt said before pausing. "Look, this mission is a two-for-one deal. We need you to shut down this mining operation, but there's something else you can do for us."

"A favor?"

"You could call it that, but one that will potentially save the lives of hundreds if not thousands of people."

"And what does this entail?"

"There were a couple of long range missiles that were recently stolen from a South African military base—and these missiles need to be retrieved."

"What's wrong with the South Africans? Can't they go after their own weapons?"

"Their special ops forces—the Recces—could, but we believe it might be held by Demby and his outfit as well. This operation needs to be done discreetly and all at once if we want to shut him down for good."

"And you expect me to retrieve long-range missiles on my own?"

"A tactical team will secure them once you've completed your task. But before you go, there's someone you need to meet who can fill you in on all the details of that side of the mission—and even provide you with some valuable tech to help you succeed."

Hawk felt a fish strike his line. He fought the fish for about a minute before reeling in a five-pound bass. He pulled the hook out of its mouth and released it back into the water. Standing up, he turned around and looked at Blunt. "Who do you want me to meet?"

"Tom Colton."

CHAPTER 2

ALEX AGREED DUNCAN ENJOYED TOYING with the CIA ever since they kicked her out. Her favorite trick was to hack into the agency's servers and let the geniuses in cyber security follow her digital trail back to CIA Director Simon Coker's home computer. No matter how many times she did this, she couldn't wipe the smile off her face the entire time she was rooting around in their system for information. But tonight was different. Even though she made it look like the hack was coming from Coker, she stopped smiling seconds into her undertaking when she realized she'd never find the files on their servers.

You've gotta be kidding me.

She slammed her laptop down and let out a long string of expletives. She'd promised Hawk she'd look into the truth about his father and who he really was. And it would've been easy with the information given to her. Simply look up the name "Franklin Foster" and sift through his files. But there was only one file on him—and it stated that all files on Foster were archived in The Vault. That was the CIA's way of saying that either they hadn't gotten around to digitizing the files yet or they were so sensitive that they'd never be put on a server for fear that someone might hack the information. Based on how dodgy Blunt had been about Hawk's father, she assumed it was the latter.

Her phone rang, jolting her out of her dazed trance.

"What'd you find?" Hawk asked once she answered the phone.

"You're not gonna believe this."

"Try me."

She took a deep breath. "All the files on your father are in The Vault."

"*The Vault?*"

"Yeah, the CIA's high security archives, *that* vault." She paused. "It'll just make things a little more challenging for me, but I'm up for the task."

"You're not seriously considering breaking in there are you?"

"Nope. I'm not considering it—I'm doing it."

"Alex, I appreciate all you're doing for me, I really do. But that's not worth the risk. What if you get caught? It's not exactly the kind of place they'll just slap you on the wrist and let you go."

"Don't I know that all too well?"

"Coker kicked you out and black balled you. What do you think he's going to do if he finds out that you tried to infiltrate The Vault?"

"He doesn't scare me."

"Well, he should." Hawk took a deep breath. "I just can't in good conscience let you go do something like that for me."

"You don't have to let me do anything because I'm doing it on my own volition. Besides, I'm too interested in this case now just to drop it."

"Just rethink this Alex, okay? Blunt will go ballistic if he finds out."

"Do you plan on telling him?"

"No."

"Good because I don't plan on getting caught either."

"You got a way in?"

"Do I ever."

NEWSLETTER SIGNUP

If you would like to stay up to date on R.J. Patterson's latest writing projects with his periodic newsletter, visit his website at www.RJPbooks.com.

ABOUT THE AUTHOR

R.J. PATTERSON is an award-winning writer living in southeastern Idaho. He first began his illustrious writing career as a sports journalist, recording his exploits on the soccer fields in England as a young boy. Then when his father told him that people would pay him to watch sports if he would write about what he saw, he went all in. He landed his first writing job at age 15 as a sports writer for a daily newspaper in Orangeburg, S.C. He later attended earned a degree in newspaper journalism from the University of Georgia, where he took a job covering high school sports for the award-winning *Athens Banner-Herald* and *Daily News*.

He later became the sports editor of *The Valdosta Daily Times* before working in the magazine world as an editor and freelance journalist. He has won numerous writing awards, including a national award for his investigative reporting on a sordid tale surrounding an

NCAA investigation over the University of Georgia football program.

R.J. enjoys the great outdoors of the Northwest while living there with his wife and three children. He still follows sports closely.

He also loves connecting with readers and would love to hear from you. To stay updated about future projects, connect with him over Facebook or on the interwebs at www.RJPbooks.com and sign up for his newsletter to get deals and updates.

Made in the USA
Middletown, DE
18 November 2018